Wendy Etherington

HER PRIVATE TREASURE

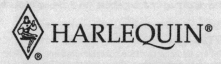

TORONTO • NEW YORK • LONDON
AMSTERDAM • PARIS • SYDNEY • HAMBURG
STOCKHOLM • ATHENS • TOKYO • MILAN • MADRID
PRAGUE • WARSAW • BUDAPEST • AUCKLAND

Recycling programs
for this product may
not exist in your area.

ISBN-13: 978-0-373-79566-6

HER PRIVATE TREASURE

ABOUT THE AUTHOR

Wendy Etherington was born and raised in the deep South—and she has the fried chicken recipes and NASCAR ticket stubs to prove it. The author of more than twenty books, she writes full-time from her home in South Carolina, where she lives with her husband, two daughters and an energetic shih tzu named Cody. She can be reached via her Web site, www.wendyetherington.com.

Books by Wendy Etherington

HARLEQUIN BLAZE
263—JUST ONE TASTE...
310—A BREATH AWAY
385—WHAT HAPPENED
      IN VEGAS...
446—AFTER DARK
524—TEMPT ME AGAIN

HARLEQUIN NASCAR
HOT PURSUIT
FULL THROTTLE
NO HOLDING BACK,
   with Liz Allison
RISKING HER HEART,
   with Liz Allison

To my best buds, Jacquie D'Alessandro
and Jenni Grizzle, whose love, support
and interventions of champagne
and chocolate keep me sane.

1

CARR HAMILTON YANKED the rope around the dock post, then stepped off his thirty-seven-foot cabin cruiser, *The Litigator*. As rippling waves of the Intracoastal Waterway lapped against the dock, the moon hung above the marina, a glowing orb casting a cool and mysterious light. The air smelled of sea life and salt.

The gloomy night and deserted dock, plus yet another solitary cruise, had put him in a rare melancholy mood. After securing his boat, he zipped his jacket against the cool March wind and headed across the creaky wooden slats, intending to circumvent the marina bar, where he'd find friends and conversation.

"...coffee is ready for distribution, so don't get jumpy now."

Carr stopped at the familiar voice, delivered in an angry and demanding tone. Coffee distribution? Jack Rafton was an insurance agent. Auto, home, life, et cetera. Mundane stuff really. But a nice guy and good business neighbor.

"This whole thing is getting dicey," another, but unknown, voice whispered harshly.

"Relax, and keep your voices down," said yet a third man.

Carr's low mood vanished. His pulse jumped. He leaped sideways and ducked behind a large storage locker at the dock's edge, realizing he probably hadn't moved so swiftly or stealthily since his days on the Yale fencing team.

"It's late." Jack's voice again. "Locals are all deep into their whiskey and beer by now."

"Let's just make the exchange and get out of here." The second unknown voice.

"You're just pissed I raised my prices," Jack said.

"Whatever," the first unknown man said, his voice deep and raspy. A smoker maybe. "That's between you and the boss. Just give us the stuff."

Carr heard footsteps on the wooden slats, then the creak of a rope tethering a boat.

He risked a glance from behind the post and saw Jack carrying a wooden crate and walking slow, balanced steps on the deck of a ski boat. By the blue and red stripes on the hull, it appeared to be Jack's boat, but it was too dark to make out the name scripted on the side and be certain.

The crate was handed over to one of the two unidentified men, then something was shoved into Jack's hand. All the characters stood in shadow, like the old black-and-white film noirs Carr enjoyed. He half expected to see Humphrey Bogart's strong-jawed profile flash before him.

No hat-and-raincoat-clad detectives appeared, so Carr concentrated on what he could see. The two unknown men scurried away from Jack and the boat. He tried to estimate their height and weight, but knew both were wild guesses based on a comparison of Jack's vital statistics.

Jack transferred the object he'd been given—an envelope maybe?—to his other hand, then, suddenly, he turned in Carr's direction. Fairly certain the angle and the width of the post kept him hidden, Carr didn't move. He barely breathed. Whatever the meeting with the two men meant, Carr knew it wasn't something Jack wanted known by a business acquaintance. The timing as well as the conversation itself spoke to that certainty.

After a few moments, he heard Jack's footsteps receding down the dock. He counted slowly to a hundred before moving and then only to take a quick look. Noting the dock was empty, he shifted from his position.

Puzzling over the discussion he'd heard, he checked his boat to be sure he'd locked the cabin door and secured the rope properly. The exchange had to be a payoff of some kind. The two men had clearly bought something from Jack. But coffee? Why would three men need to meet in the dead of night to buy and sell coffee?

He walked down the dock, stopping as he reached the boat Jack had retrieved the crate from. *American Dream* was clearly scripted on the hull in bright red letters. Jack's boat, then.

Stooping, Carr glided his hand over the dock's rough wooden planks. Something gritty caressed the tips of his fingers. He brought his hand to his face, inhaling the scent. Coffee.

With the scent, he recalled one significant reason coffee grounds might be placed in a crate, then traded for cash in the dead of night.

Drugs.

Two weeks later

FBI SPECIAL AGENT Malina Blair glared at the stack of case files on her desk and thought seriously about pulling her pistol from its ever-present side holster and firing at will.

Two computer hacking cases, one suspected drug smuggling and six complaints from helpful citizens who thought they spotted someone from the Most Wanted list hiding out behind the fake designer bags in the straw market.

How far the mighty had fallen.

She recalled fondly the business executive son's kidnapping case she'd closed three years ago. She supposed the son and his loved ones didn't remember the ordeal in a positive light, but the family still sent her a Christmas card every year, thanking her for her sharpshooting skills.

And barely six months ago, she'd led a team in solving a six-year-old bank robbery, taking down the ring of suspects as they attempted to break into the main branch vault of the Bank of America in downtown Washington, D.C.

Good times. Career-making moments.

Formally interviewing Senator Phillip Grammer's son on suspicion of securities and bank fraud hadn't gone quite so well. The powerful politician had stormed into the interview and claimed his son had fallen in with the wrong crowd briefly and that he and the SEC were working out a special process of restitution.

Phil junior was special all right. He'd ratted on three other people—who Malina considered minor players in the deal—and got away scot-free.

While a lovely city, Charleston, South Carolina,

wasn't exactly the FBI's hotbed of excitement. Getting back to headquarters in Quantico, Virginia, was imperative, especially since screwing up again was likely to land her reassigned in the desert-to-nowhere field office. Interrogating cacti.

With a sigh, she pulled out the folder about the smuggling case. Her boss had actually dropped this one on her desk that morning. At first, she'd hoped she'd been forgiven for her career-crushing mistake and assigned to the elite team that worked the harbor. With the Port of Charleston being the country's fourth busiest, illicit goods and terrorist threats were a serious possibility.

Unfortunately, the case she'd been assigned was a vague suspicion of drug smuggling based on a two-minute overheard conversation that took place on nearby—and boringly tiny—Palmer's Island. The single witness was an attorney and friend of her boss.

It seemed she had another day of tedium ahead of her.

Scooping up the documents, she headed out of her cubicle and toward the elevator.

"Hey, Malina," Donald, one of her colleagues, called out as she passed his cube. "Gonna work another dog-napping case today?"

She never slowed her brisk stride as she called back, "I'll see if I can fit it in after kicking your ass in combat training this afternoon."

"Again," several others called out helpfully from behind their own cubicle walls.

She lifted her lips in what some people might consider a sneer, but those who knew her recognized it as her version of a smile. She'd only been in the Charleston field office three weeks, and while everyone knew of her setback, most had at least come to respect her skills and determination. Hers was a cautionary tale none of them wanted coming true in their own lives.

Alone in the elevator, she allowed herself the weakness of closing her eyes as frustration overcame her. She should be in a corner office with a view. She should be solving important cases. She should be compiling letters of commendation.

She was good at her job—a few she'd worked with had even called her the best. If only she had tact as steady as her hands and as sure as her roundhouse kick, she'd rise to the top.

Donald hadn't exaggerated. Her first case since arriving at the office had been a literal dog-napping.

The mayor's prize Maltese had gone missing, and a ransom demand had been made. It had taken her all of two minutes in an interview with the dog walker to crack him and the master plot.

The mayor's kids had hugged her; her coworkers had laughed their asses off.

Minutes later, while she drove her government-issue sedan over the bridge to Palmer's Island, she cast a glance at the sun's rays bouncing off the rippling Atlantic waves in the distance. Ahead was Patriot's Point, where the decommissioned aircraft carrier the *USS Yorktown* had been permanently docked, awaiting the daily flood of tourists eager to explore her proud and massive decks.

The island that was her destination was even smaller than the one where she'd been raised. In fact, Kauai, Hawaii was as different from Palmer's Island as two floating rock and sand masses could be. And yet, they had the same effect—they calmed and soothed as no other person, place or thing had ever managed in her life.

She'd continue to resist her mother's assertion that someday she'd want to return home, but Palmer's Island did force her to remember that her life hadn't always been about ambition, power and politics.

She found the address she was looking for with little effort and pulled into the small sand-and-shell-dotted parking lot beside a large house that had been converted into a quad-plex of offices. A discreet sign announced Tessa Malone, Family Counselor; Jack Rafton, Island Insurance; Charlie McGary, Suncoast Real Estate; and Carr Hamilton, Attorney-at-Law.

Mr. Hamilton's office was on the lower left, across the main hall from the insurance agent, who was the primary focus in the supposed smuggling operation.

The whole case would most certainly turn out to be nothing. Rafton and Hamilton were probably involved in some minor quarrel, and this was the attorney's idea of revenge. Maybe Rafton had cut Hamilton off in traffic or carelessly blocked the driveway with cans on trash day or any number of other ridiculous things that people got worked up over.

For her, this trip was merely another hoop to jump through in order to get her career back on track.

She turned the brass knob on the door to Hamilton's office and entered to find herself in a small but elegant reception area. Malina's footsteps echoed across dark oak hardwood floors as a quick glance took in the emerald curtains, pale gold walls and expensive-looking antique furniture.

A woman with dark brown hair, streaked with silver, sat behind an antique cherry desk. She looked up with a polite smile. "May I help you?"

Malina pulled her badge from her jacket pocket.

"Special Agent Malina Blair. I have an appointment with Mr. Hamilton."

The polite smile never wavered, leading Malina to wonder if the cops came calling frequently or if she was simply unruffled by any visitor. "Of course." She lifted the phone on her desk. "I'll let him know you're here." After a brief conversation, she rose and hung up the phone. "This way, please."

The receptionist/secretary turned away toward the door in the back of the room. Her tailored brown suit showed off her trim figure, just as her matching heels highlighted her confident stride.

Malina had discovered she could glean valuable information about the person in charge by watching subordinates. If that observation held true in this case, she could expect Carr Hamilton to be self-assured, efficient and sophisticated. Not exactly what she'd expected from simple little Palmer's Island.

She followed the receptionist into the office and barely resisted gasping at the man who rose from behind the massive mahogany desk at the back of the room.

He was beautiful.

At a trim six foot two with wide shoulders and narrow hips, his body alone could cause a woman to wax poetic, something Malina never felt moved by but finally understood why others did. He wore an exquisite charcoal suit, and his thick, silky-looking, inky-black hair set off a face sculpted like the statue of an ancient god, even though nothing about him was cold.

In fact, he radiated heat—especially from his dark brown eyes, sharp and intelligent, standing out from that spectacular face, absorbing her from head to toe.

Moving gracefully, he rounded the desk and extended his hand, which was tanned and long fingered, elegant as everything around him. "Thank you for coming, Agent Blair."

Jolted into remembering she was there on a professional mission, she managed a nod as she took his hand. A shock of desire raced up her arm. "Sure thing."

His gaze lingered on her face, and she resisted the urge to pull her hand from his. There was something powerful, even meaningful, about that stare, and she didn't like the sensation that she'd lost control and perspective so quickly. In that moment, she was a woman, not an agent, and that was entirely the wrong tone for this meeting.

"Coffee, Mr. Hamilton?" the receptionist asked from behind Malina.

"Yes, Paige. Thank you. I imagine Agent Blair would prefer the Kona blend."

Paige turned and left the room, presumably to get coffee, and Malina forced herself to both step back from Hamilton's enticing touch and simultaneously hang on to his compelling gaze. "Kona?" she asked.

"You are Hawaiian, aren't you?"

"Yes."

She clenched her back teeth to avoid asking him how he knew her heritage, but he simply nodded in response to the unspoken question.

"I'm good with faces." He extended his hand to one of the club chairs in front of his desk, then returned to his position on the other side, lowering himself into his blood-red leather chair only after she'd done the same. "Also, Sam mentioned you'd grown up on Kauai."

Gorgeous, intelligent and honest. Three very good reasons to get to know a man. Unfortunately, he was part of her professional and not her personal life.

And never the twain shall meet.

She'd seen too many careers wither and die from office bed-hopping. And falling into the wrong bed in the world of politics landed the offenders a one-way ticket to early retirement. No way was she going down that road.

"I understand the SAC is a personal friend," she said, leaning back in the club chair and tucking her neglected libido neatly away.

He nodded. "Special Agent in Charge Samuel Clairmont." He lifted his lips in a smile that made Malina's heart jump. "He's come a long way from third string on the Yale fencing team."

"I guess you were first-string."

"Of course."

From any other man, that admission would be bragging at best, pretentious at worst. In the capable, elegant hands of Carr Hamilton, it was charming.

Paige returned at that moment with a silver tray, holding a pitcher, mugs and tiny silver spoons.

She set the service on Hamilton's desk, then turned and left the room. As he poured the coffee, Malina took a moment to let her gaze roam the office, noting the dark wood floor-to-ceiling bookcases filled with volumes, a few pictures and knickknacks. A wide-screen laptop sat on the left side of his desk. A sideboard served as a bar, displaying cut-crystal glasses and decanters filled with amber liquid.

Class, style and old money permeated the room.

"Cream and sugar?" the man across from her asked.

She almost said yes simply to watch those graceful hands move. "No, thank you."

"Strong coffee for a strong woman."

Since she had no idea what to say to that statement

without heading the conversation down a personal path, she sipped from her mug. The Kona was bold and flavorful, just as it should be.

He looked amused as he settled back into his chair, no doubt realizing she was attracted to him. A man with his looks and style wouldn't miss such an obvious detail.

Despite the near certain futility and mundane nature of her task, she had to be careful not to take the wrong step with this man. He stirred something in her better left unturned. She had a singular goal and couldn't afford any distraction.

But she so hated being careful.

"So, what do you think of my observations?" he asked.

"I'm not sure what to think at this point. I'd like you to tell me what you saw in detail." From her pocket, she pulled out a microrecorder, which she set on the desk in front of him. "For the record." She recited the standard warning about testimony and giving false information to law enforcement, then settled back to listen.

He gave a report as organized and detailed as any cop. He was careful not to speculate and left out personal feelings, as she would expect from a lawyer. From the file the SAC had given her, she'd read about his success litigating civil cases in a variety of antitrust suits, products liability and environmental issues. She could well imagine him living like a king on the proceeds of his powerful voice and structured mind.

Still, the likelihood of an everyday citizen cracking a drug-smuggling operation was about as likely as her suddenly deciding to lay down her Glock and become a pole dancer.

"Drugs are smuggled in coffee grounds," he said in conclusion.

"Twenty years ago," she said drily as she turned off the recorder and returned it to her pocket. "Things have gotten a bit more sophisticated these days."

"I don't envision Jack as a major drug kingpin. This is a small operation. Unsophisticated methods would suit them better."

Despite herself, she was impressed he'd thought through the conclusions of what he'd witnessed. "So why did you come to us? If Rafton is dealing drugs, this is a matter for the DEA."

"I have reason to believe he's smuggling more than drugs."

"How?" she asked, though she suddenly knew.

"I've been watching him."

She sighed heavily. Random citizens playing at being cops was a surefire way of getting somebody killed. "I'd prefer you leave this to the professionals."

"You mean the professionals who don't believe anything illicit is going on?"

"I haven't come to any conclusions yet."

Clearly annoyed, he tapped his fingers against the arm of his chair. His gaze locked with hers. "The FBI do investigate major thefts, don't they?"

"Last time I checked."

"And art theft would still fall in that category?"

"It would."

"Then I've come to the right agency."

It would still mean she'd have to give the DEA a heads-up, and interjurisdictional cooperation with those cowboys was one of her least favorite job requirements.

Hamilton leaned forward. "I didn't ask you here on a

whim, Agent Blair. I'm not a panicked or bored islander looking for attention. There's something to this case."

"It's not a case yet."

Those elegant hands, linked and resting on the desk in front of him, clenched. "Why are you so skeptical of my information?"

"Why do you think Jack Rafton's stealing art?"

"Because two nights ago, he unloaded a box shaped like a large painting."

She'd asked the obvious; she'd gotten the obvious answer. "Maybe he's just buying art with his drug-smuggling proceeds."

"Maybe he is. Why are you so skeptical of my information?"

Because the SAC would never, on purpose, give me anything with teeth.

She bit back that response, though, and stated facts, which she was sure the sharp lawyer would appreciate. "Drug smuggling is an extremely risky and dangerous pastime. Only the very desperate or very foolish would choose that route. The drug kingpins are protective to the death of their product's distribution and often disembowel those who cross them.

"From the quick background check I did on Jack Rafton, summa cum laude graduate of the College of Charleston and longtime insurance broker of Palmer's Island, I don't see him blending well in that violent world."

Hamilton nodded. "True enough."

"Rafton also doesn't drive an exotic car, which, if you'll pardon the cliché, is a drug dealer's biggest weakness."

"And how do you know that?"

She shrugged. "The parking lot outside. There's a

well-used SUV that belongs to the family counselor. A fairly new but understated luxury sedan for the real estate agent, a pickup truck for the insurance guy and a perfectly restored Triumph Spitfire convertible painted British Racing Green." She lifted her eyebrows. "Which I'm sure belongs to you."

"You ran the tags."

"Didn't need to."

He said nothing for a long moment as he studied her. "Well, I suppose somebody at the Bureau is taking my suspicions seriously if they sent you."

She started to argue with him, to explain that the only reason she'd been sent was because he was friends with a powerful man. But admitting that would be admitting she had no influence and simply did as she was told. Plus, despite the urge not to be, she was flattered he recognized her investigative skills.

"We appreciate the cooperation of concerned citizens and follow up on any tip that will lead to the arrest and conviction of anyone participating in criminal activity."

"Ah, the pat, politically correct answer. Not what I would have expected from a woman who risked her career by questioning Senator Grammer's son."

Malina felt the blood drain from her head as humiliation washed over her. "Agent Clairmont told you."

Hamilton nodded. "As I'm sure he mentioned, we're old friends. For what it's worth, he considers you an asset to the Bureau. He also respects your willingness to do whatever it takes to see justice served, even if your methods are sometimes rash."

"That kid was guilty as sin," she said, fighting to talk past her tight jaw, even as she felt a quick spurt of pleasure in hearing her boss respected her.

"Sam thinks so, too. Power buys silence way too easily."

"Not with me."

"So noted. But I'm guessing a drug- and/or art-smuggling case could put a nice letter of commendation in your file. Not to mention I'm suddenly moved to make a generous campaign donation to whoever runs against that idiot Grammer in the next election."

Her gaze shot to his. "Surely you didn't just attempt to bribe a government agent."

A wide, breath-stealing smile bloomed on his face. "Surely not."

She rose slowly to her feet. Who the hell was this guy?

Smart, successful and wealthy. A law-abiding citizen who took untold hours of his time to investigate a professional neighbor, then used a powerful association to see that his observations were taken seriously. Was he bored, curious or did he have a hidden agenda?

Bracing her hands on his desk, she noted he'd stood when she had and now she was forced to look up at him. At five-seven, she wasn't a tiny woman, but the height and breadth of him made her feel small and feminine in comparison. "I'm here to follow up on your information as ordered by my supervisor, Special Agent in Charge Samuel Clairmont. Do you have anything further to add to your previous statements?"

"I imagine you'd be interested in the storage garage Jack keeps under an assumed name in Charleston, which currently houses a brand-new Lotus Elise."

"How do you—" She stopped, shaking her head, irritated that he'd, yet again, managed to surprise her. "You followed him."

"I'd also like to point out that he chose Ardent Red

instead of British Racing Green for the exterior paint."
He cocked his head. "Do you think that's an indicator
of law-abiding citizen versus master smuggler?"

Temper brought heat to her cheeks. "Mr. Hamilton,
I'm—"

"Call me Carr."

"*Mr. Hamilton,* I'm advising—no," she amended,
"I'm *ordering* you to bring your amateur investigation
to a halt. Do not question Mr. Rafton or his associates.
Do not ask others about him and definitely do not follow
him. The Bureau will look into your information and
take things from here."

"But you don't really believe me."

"I do, in fact. I trust that you saw what you say you
have. What those observations mean is an entirely different subject." She reached into her pocket for a business card, which she laid on his desk to avoid touching
him again. It seemed imperative that she get away from
this man as fast as possible. "Let me know if I can be of
further assistance." She turned, then paused and glanced
back. "Or if you find Jimmy Hoffa."

With that parting shot, she headed toward the door,
longing to run when she sensed him following her. She
caught a whiff of his cologne, a blend of sandalwood
and amber, as warm and enticing as the man himself.

Her hand was on the doorknob when he spoke. "Professional considerations aside, I'd like to take you to
dinner sometime."

Swallowing hard, she forced herself to meet his gaze.
"Sorry. You're a witness. I'm not allowed."

"But you're not even certain a crime has been
committed."

Despite what she'd told him and the sheer unlikelihood of anything significant happening on Palmer's

Island, she knew there was. Her instincts were buzzing, and they hadn't steered her wrong yet.

Well, except for that senatorial questioning thing.

"I'm investigating," she said shortly, hoping to further discourage him.

Either he didn't get the signal or he didn't care, since he reached out, sliding his fingertip along her jaw, sending waves of heat racing down her body. "And I imagine you don't give a damn about what's allowed."

Her breath caught. She didn't. At least she never had.

And look where that attitude had led you.

Opening the door, she stepped out of his reach. "I also don't have time to get involved. I'm going to close as many cases as I can and get back to D.C., where I belong, as soon as possible."

Disappointment moved across his handsome face. He slid his hands into the pockets of his suit pants. "Of course," he said quietly. "Thanks for coming."

She regretted her abrupt tone but didn't see how she could change what was. "One last thing about Rafton." Though she already knew the answer, caution demanded she ask. "This isn't personal, right? Rafton didn't hit your car or steal your girlfriend?"

"No. And I don't have a girlfriend." His dark eyes gleamed with power and possession. "If I did, neither Jack Rafton nor any other man would take her."

2

As Carr sipped his whiskey at The Night Heron bar, he watched out the back windows as boats docked and launched for sunset cruises down the Intracoastal Waterway, then rounded the tip of the island and out into the Atlantic.

Had he finally spent too much time slowing down and reflecting?

Observation had become a staple. Watching other people do interesting things.

For so many years, he'd been on the fast track. He'd spent every waking moment establishing a lucrative practice in Manhattan, fighting for clients with prospects for big payoffs, dismissing others he might have helped but whose cases weren't as profitable.

He'd dispassionately profited from suffering and built a fortune and fierce reputation by doing so.

He hadn't paused to notice small, everyday things. To stroll the beaches he'd grown up on. To appreciate love and friendship. To watch the birds glide across the night sky.

It had taken the death of his uncle and mentor to jolt him.

Uncle Clinton had departed his life respected, rich and bitterly alone. He'd coldly extracted every penny from every case he'd taken on. He'd corrupted idealistic law school graduates with promises of wealth and power. Few, other than the descendants who inherited his money, had mourned him.

As Carr had watched heaps of fertile earth drop onto his uncle's casket, he knew he was destined for the same end. And he knew he had to find another path.

That had been two years ago, and while he didn't regret finding his roots again and settling on quiet Palmer's Island, the sparks of need for excitement came more frequently these days.

Dear heaven, did he have to fade into tedium? Was that his penance?

"*Hel-lo,* gorgeous."

Certain he wasn't being addressed, Carr nevertheless glanced at Jimmy, The Heron's weekday bartender, and noted his gaze locked on the door behind Carr. "What hot blonde are you fixated on tonight?"

"Brunette," he returned, his eyes following the subject in question.

Carr didn't bother to turn. Being barely twenty-one, Jimmy's taste inevitably skewed young. At thirty-five, Carr wasn't even remotely swimming in the same pool.

Instead, he stared at his whiskey.

"What are you doing here?" a familiar voice asked seconds later.

Raising his head, Carr blinked, but Special Agent Malina Blair was still sliding onto the bar stool next to him, changing his evening from watchful boredom to stimulating possibility in a matter of seconds.

"Drinking." He raised his glass as he absorbed her lovely features. "Join me?"

Her exotic turquoise gaze slid from his face to his glass and back again. "Why the hell not?"

He only had to lift his finger to get Jimmy assembling her drink. "I like you a lot better when you're speaking your mind instead of spouting Bureau platitudes." Not that he hadn't liked her then as well. His fingers tingled with the urge to pull her silky-looking dark hair from the restraining ponytail secured at the base of her neck. "How's the investigation progressing?"

"I would like you a lot better if you'd stay out of my case," she said as Jimmy set the drink before her.

"So now it's a case?"

She rolled her shoulders. "It is."

He'd had faith in her sense of justice, but he was relieved to have the instinct confirmed. Sam had been right in that she was the agent for the job.

Did his good deed erase one of the black marks next to his name?

He wasn't sure—especially since his greatest desire was to seduce her into compromising her professional code of ethics and sleeping with him.

She sipped her drink, never wincing.

Though he considered his brand of imported whiskey smooth, he knew plenty of people who found it too bracing. Women mostly. But then Malina Blair was tougher than the exotic island beauty she appeared to be.

"You like whiskey?" he asked her, fascinated by the way her pillowy lips cupped the crystal.

"Not especially." She rattled the ice in her glass.

"This is nice, though. Stop me if I lose my senses and have the urge to shoot somebody."

"I'm here to serve. Lousy day?"

"Lousy month."

"I imagine so. But do you define yourself completely by your job?"

"Yes," she said without hesitation.

That path led nowhere, as Carr well knew. She'd be so much happier if she fell into bed with him. He wondered how long it would take him to manage it.

Certainly the key to this lady's heart wouldn't be found in candy, flowers and suggestive compliments. "So I assume you've spent the last thirty-six hours pursuing the case. What have you learned?"

"That boat captains on small islands like to gossip, and your friend Jack Rafton is well liked, even if he has been coming and going at odd hours lately."

"Which you already knew by talking to me."

She shrugged. "Corroboration was necessary."

He was dying to watch that cool nonchalance fall away with the right touch. Because beneath the frustrated heat under her staid, navy-blue suit, the fire of a passionate woman lurked.

With effort, he managed to focus on their conversation. "If you need more details, you might talk to the harbormaster, Albert Duffy. He knows everything about everyone. Though you'd do better to charm him than flash your badge."

She looked at him, then glanced at her watch with a sigh. "I have a meeting with Albert Duffy in twenty minutes."

Carr tracked his gaze slowly down her body. "Not that I don't think you look amazing—and I believe

Jimmy is impressed as well—you'd do better showing Al a little leg."

She bared her teeth. "I could always show him the wrong side of a federal interrogation room."

He leaned toward her, lowering his voice several pitches. "Subtlety often works better than force."

Her gaze moved to his and held. Desire lingered in the depth of her eyes, clear as the tropical water they mimicked. Her beautiful lips parted, and for a moment, her gaze dropped to his mouth, and he thought she was going to give in to the need so obviously pulsing between them.

Tedium had vanished the moment she'd appeared, and the sensation was heady.

"Who's Jimmy?" she asked, leaning back and breaking the spell.

"The bartender." Carr inclined his head toward the young man pouring vodka in a glass for another customer. "Wave. I think he has a crush on you."

She never looked in Jimmy's direction but said, "He's too young. What are you doing here anyway?"

"Drinking, as I said earlier. But also volunteering to be your assistant, guarding your virtue, so to speak, as well as helping break the ice with Al. I'm one of the few people he actually likes."

"I thought I told you to stay out of this case."

"It's my bar."

"Literally?"

"Yes, plus I live across the street."

Admiration sparked in her eyes. "The house on the point."

"How did you know?"

She drained the rest of her drink. "It's you."

"You're hedging. You've certainly run a deep search

on me by now. You know my address, my background, my professional history and financial status. I bet you even know what grade I received on my contract law midterm my junior year of college and whether I prefer boxers or briefs. Before you walked through the door, you knew I owned this place. Why the subterfuge? Why pretend surprise at finding me here?"

"I live for subterfuge," she scoffed.

"Stop," he said quietly but firmly. The sarcasm was a defense mechanism that she obviously used to keep people from probing too deeply. A way of maintaining distance. "It wouldn't kill you to accept my help."

"No, but it might compromise my case. Plus…"

When she stopped, he prompted, "Plus?"

"I don't understand your motives. Why are you going to all this trouble? Why do you want to get involved in this investigation? What's in it for you?"

She didn't trust him. Not surprising, since he didn't trust himself. The bribery attempt, a remnant of his old ways, had been a huge misstep. But he'd wanted to know what kind of agent he was dealing with, despite Sam's assurances that Malina was fiercely ethical.

"It's my duty," he said finally.

"As what?"

"A citizen of the United States."

She shook her head. "Nobody's that committed and idealistic."

"But they should be." And he was fighting every day to be sure he could count himself among those who were. "This is my island." When she raised her eyebrows, he added, "Not all of it, though I do own a fair collection of properties. I mean, this is my birthplace, my home. It's lovely and peaceful, the place where I intend to raise my children and live until I'm ancient and dotty. I care what happens here, and I won't let smuggling or drugs or anything else ruin my community."

Saying nothing, she held his gaze. "You're—"

"Agent Blair?" a gruff voice interrupted.

Malina rose and held out her hand to harbormaster Albert Duffy. "Mr. Duffy, thanks for agreeing to meet me."

Though he shook her hand briefly, his thick gray brows drew together, and the wrinkles on his darkly tanned and lined face seemed to deepen. "I don't like working with women."

"I don't like working with anybody. Why don't we take that table in the back corner?" she suggested.

Al scowled briefly, but must have been somewhat satisfied with Malina's direct answer, because he shrugged and wandered toward the booth.

Malina turned back to Carr and spoke in a low tone only he could hear. "That was a pretty impassioned speech earlier. I can see why you were a prize to juries. I still have to ask you to keep your distance from this case." When he started to interrupt, she held up her hand to stall him. "I'd be interested in calling you for an occasional consultation, but that's where your involvement ends. Understand?"

"Since you're articulate, and I'm fairly intelligent, yes, I understand."

She narrowed her eyes briefly, as if trying to figure out if there was a loophole. Which, of course, there was.

"Your offer to help is admirable," she said after a moment. "In fact, it's—" She stopped and shook her head ruefully. "It's been a long time since I've heard sentiment like that." She brushed her hand across his arm. "Thanks."

Now she thought he was being noble.

He almost wished he could call back his words. His nobility was tainted. He didn't deserve her admiration. But he wanted her.

When she reached into her pocket and pulled out a clip of cash, he held up his hand. "I'll pay for the drinks."

"I appreciate the offer, but you can't." She took out a twenty-dollar bill and laid it on the bar.

"Generous."

She turned toward the booth Al had settled into. "My compensation to the cute bartender whose flirting I'd never consider returning."

"Why not?"

She flicked him a glance. "I'm attracted to men, not boys."

"WOULD YOU LIKE a drink, Mr. Duffy?" Malina asked as she scooted into the booth and faced the cranky harbormaster.

He pointed a knobby finger toward the bar area. "It's comin'."

Malina looked over to see Carr Hamilton headed toward them, a glass of whiskey in each hand.

He slid onto the seat beside Duffy, then lifted his drink in a toast and his lips in smirk. "I figured you'd want to abstain. On duty and all."

"Very considerate, Mr. Hamilton," she said, certain the sharp attorney caught her sarcasm. "However, I don't need your assistance."

"I'm sure you don't. However, I'm Mr. Duffy's lawyer."

"He called you?"

"No, but isn't it fortunate I was here? I'll stay on his behalf."

"I don't want to be here at all," Duffy said, glaring at her.

"Me either," she muttered. The man she had the reluctant hots for was currently sitting across from her, meddling in her case, distracting her from nearly everything. "But I have a job to do."

Duffy sipped his drink. "You should be home, cookin' for your man."

Though her muscles tensed like a coiled snake, she managed to let the anger roll off. "I'm better with a pistol than a spatula."

"Not natural," Duffy insisted.

Malina drilled her gaze into his. "Frankly, Mr. Duffy, I'd rather be anywhere else, talking to anyone else than you. And yet…" She lifted her hands and leaned back. "Here I am, striving to protect the law-abiding citizens of Palmer's Island from the criminal element. If I can make the sacrifice, so can you."

Duffy continued to glare silently at her, as if sure he'd never seen a self-possessed woman in his life.

"Al," Hamilton said quietly, "let her do this."

Duffy sighed. "Yeah, okay."

"I'd like to record the interview, if that's okay with you." She cast Hamilton a glance. "And your attorney, of course." With their verbal agreements secured, she asked Duffy, "Do you know Jack Rafton?"

Duffy looked wary. "Yeah. Slip number nine."

"Owner of a twenty-six-foot cabin cruiser called *American Dream*?"

"Yeah."

"How would you characterize your relationship?"

"We ain't got a relationship, lady. We're men."

And not homophobic at all. Malina resisted the urge to roll her eyes. She liked her job, she really did. Or, rather, she used to. "Are you friends?" she asked.

Duffy shrugged. "We have a drink together sometimes."

"Have you ever been to his house?"

"No."

"Do you have his cell phone number?"

"No."

"What do you talk about when you're together?"

"Fishing. What does that have to do with anything?"

"She's trying to determine if you're close friends with Jack," Hamilton put in.

"Are you?" Malina pressed the harbormaster.

"I guess not."

The man could give clams pointers. "But you see Mr. Rafton frequently."

"He has a boat. I run the harbor."

"Does Mr. Rafton seem under an unusual amount of stress lately?"

"How the hell do I know?"

"Have you seen him at the docks at unusual times over the last few weeks?"

Duffy's gaze darted to Hamilton. "What does she mean *unusual?*"

Hamilton's lips twitched. "Out of the ordinary."

"I know that. I don't know what that has to do with—"

"You run the harbor," Malina interrupted. "You know when people come and go. When does Rafton usually come and go?"

"Early morning, sometimes after dinner."

"When has he been taking his boat out lately?"

Duffy sipped his whiskey before answering. "Later."

"How much later?"

"Eleven, maybe twelve at night."

"So would you characterize that as unusual?"

Annoyance lined Duffy's face. "I guess so."

His statement fell in line with what others had said with less reluctance and certainly more grace. Was Albert Duffy simply ornery, or did he have some connection with Rafton that he didn't want known? With this man, directness seemed to be the only course. "Are you engaging in or helping to cover up illegal activity perpetrated by Jack Rafton?"

Duffy sputtered so heavily he couldn't speak.

"Agent Blair," Hamilton said, his gaze locking on hers, "that's inappropriate."

But it confirmed her instincts—Duffy was an insulting curmudgeon and likely not a would-be felon.

"I thought we might get to our goal more quickly with more specific questions," she said to the men across from her. "And I'm sure Mr. Duffy doesn't think the FBI engages in random questioning. I wanted to let him know that he's being watched and any attempt by him to warn Mr. Rafton of the questions I've asked would be perceived by me as the act of an accomplice." She smiled. "Everybody clear now?"

"What a man does on his own time isn't any of my bother," Duffy mumbled.

Her smile broadened. "Exactly. That's my job. Thank you for your assistance, Mr. Duffy," she added, rising and turning off the microrecorder. "I'll forward copies of the interview transcript to your office, Mr. Hamilton. Good night to you both."

"You'd do better to learn to cook, honey," Duffy said as she turned away.

Facing him, her fingers twitched as she skimmed her hand across the butt of her gun. "Would I?"

"Yeah." His gaze defiant, Duffy leaned back in the booth. "Carr here needs a girlfriend. He's rich, so he could probably even get you lessons."

"If only I'd known those options were open to me, I'd have skipped training in Quantico and raced right over to the Julia Child Institute." Her temper finally breaking, she braced her palm on the table and leaned toward Duffy, meeting his startled gaze with her own furious, narrowed one. "As it happens, I'm a pretty good ass-kicker, so I think I'll stick with what I know." She paused briefly, renewing her smile, even though it was significantly cooler. "As long as that's okay with you."

Stalking away, she didn't dare look at Hamilton, who'd no doubt find a way to warm her icy demeanor.

Chauvinistic, patronizing men who were threatened by women in general, not just the ones carrying firearms, didn't warrant any room in her thoughts. And yet, here she was, striding to her car and dwelling on the interview as if she cared whether or not she could boil water.

If Duffy owned a gun, it was doubtful he'd be able to hit the broad side of a barn with it, even with a sniper's scope and a GPS. And yet nobody was questioning his ability to be harbormaster. Though what his job had to do with weapons, she couldn't say. She just—

She ground to a halt next to her dark blue sedan. Those two didn't seriously think the investigation of this case would be reduced to gender, did they? Suspected smuggling was serious business that had nothing to do with chromosomes.

Frankly, she'd expected better from Carr Hamilton.

He caught up to her in the parking lot, bracing his arm on the hood of her car and standing way too close. "Why did you come here tonight?"

Again, she was conscious of feeling small. As an agent, the sensation bothered her. As a woman, she couldn't help inhaling his cologne's spicy scent and spending a few seconds reveling in the head-spinning that followed.

She told herself it was important that she stand her ground and resist his advances. If she let him inside, she wasn't sure how she could stay objective. Stepping back, she rolled her shoulders. "I'm here because this is where Duffy wanted to meet. He's a complete ass, by the way."

"I did advise you to show some leg."

Briefly, she closed her eyes to get a better handle on her temper. Was he really just like everybody else? "You don't honestly believe I'd resort to low-cut dresses or high heels to solve my case," she said, her gaze boring into his.

"Sure I do." He closed the distance she'd created between them. "If it solved your case, you'd do just about anything."

His assured tone angered her—or so she tried to convince herself. The fact that his statement was true was irrelevant.

Hamilton cocked his head. "As far as your personal life, though, I think you'd make a man's journey just about as difficult as you could."

Also true. Though not out of any deliberate issue with

men in general—except the chauvinistic, homophobic or idiotic ones. She simply hadn't met many men worth giving her time to lately. And if she was lonely, she had her job to focus on. The SAC respected her. For now, that would have to be enough to keep the home fires burning.

She crossed her arms over her chest. "Did they teach you how to be an egomaniac at Yale?"

Ignoring her defensive stance, he leaned into her. "No, I think that particular quality is inborn."

The challenge in his dark eyes hadn't wavered once since the moment she met him.

She liked that.

Truth told, she liked him. But he was intimately involved in her case, and she knew an attraction to him wasn't wise.

"Are you sure you didn't come here to see me?" he asked.

"I came to interrogate a person of interest in my case." If she figured the owner of the bar, who she'd learned spent many of his nights in that bar, showed up, well, that was simply a side benefit to a job that had sold her short on positive points so far.

His gaze roved her face. "And I'm irrelevant?"

"You're...distracting," she admitted, her heart racing with the crazy need that she sensed would always mark any encounter with Carr Hamilton.

"Then I'm doing my job."

She angled her head. "Is that why you followed me out here—to do your job?"

His tongue moistened his lower lip, and she barely repressed a groan. "No." He wrapped one arm around her waist. "I have other things on my mind right now."

As he lowered his head, she knew she could stop him. Should stop him.

But there were times when her instincts took over, and while those interludes didn't always end the way she'd anticipated or desired, she couldn't deny they always made things interesting.

She doubted touching Carr Hamilton would be any different.

His hand cupped her jaw as he laid his mouth over hers. As his fingers gripped the back of her head, his tongue slid between her lips, sending sparks of desire and need shooting through her body. The lustful feelings smoldering inside exploded.

Their chests met; her nipples tightened.

Her body wanted him, even if her brain warned of the danger. With a moan of longing, she ignored her conscience. She clutched the front of his shirt as he continued to devour her mouth, seeming determined to absorb every part of her into him, and she was willing to let him.

Willing? Hell, she wanted more.

Much more.

He pressed her back against her car. "I've thought of nothing but you since yesterday," he rasped in her ear.

Her pulse hammered. Her body throbbed.

Different didn't even begin to describe the hunger pulsing through her. She'd anticipated a spark and gotten an inferno.

She pressed her lips to his throat and buried her hand in the inky locks of his hair that indeed felt like silk. "You're part of my case. I shouldn't—"

He silenced her with another kiss. Her protests died in the wake of the raw emotions consuming her. Her belly tightened, craving more of his touch, knowing instinctively he could drive away the loneliness and satisfy both her body and her mind.

She wanted his skin pressed against hers. She wanted to let loose the fire behind his dark eyes.

His hand slid up her stomach, and her breasts tingled in anticipation. But before he could reach his goal, his thumb brushed her shoulder holster.

She shoved him back instantly.

In the dimly lit parking lot, white sand beneath her shoes, ocean breeze brushing against her skin, she gasped for air and watched him. He looked as dazed as she felt.

"You touched—" She broke off and slid her hands into her pants pockets. Her fingers quivered with the need to brush an errant lock of his silky hair off his forehead. She cleared her throat and tried again. "Sorry. My weapon holster. It's an instinctive thing for a cop to protect."

Still breathing heavily, his mouth lifted on one side. "Remind me to disarm you next time."

She shook her head. There shouldn't be a next time.

And yet could she really imagine resisting the beautiful man standing before her for long? If he wanted her— and by the evidence presented in the past few minutes she could only assume he did—was there any way she wouldn't be his?

She shivered at the thought.

"Cold?" he asked, stepping forward and bracing his palms beneath her elbows.

"No." She shook her head. "That's the last thing I am."

His hands gripped her waist, and she noted he was

careful to keep them away from her holster. "Come home with me."

She turned away. "I can't. I need to think." She'd never been a coward in her life, but she wasn't sure whether she should run toward or away from this man.

"Think about me?" he asked, his lips against her ear.

"Among other things. I need to go to the gun club."

"The…what?"

She glanced over her shoulder into his confused eyes. "Gun club. They have an indoor shooting range that's open twenty-four hours." Then she remembered the whiskey she'd indulged in earlier. The club would have to wait for morning. "I like to shoot to relax."

"I like to walk on the beach."

Just another way they were opposites and completely wrong for each other.

When she opened her car door, he let go of her and stepped back. "You want a ride home?" she asked him.

He started off. "I'll walk. Thanks."

"Oh, Hamilton? By—"

"Do you think you could call me by my first name?"

"No, I really don't think I can now."

He scowled. "Then when?"

She shrugged. "When it's the right time. And, by the way…" She let her gaze track down his body, long, lean and illuminated by the streetlight. "The Bureau couldn't care less whether you wear boxers, briefs or nothing at all."

"What about you?"

She had no doubt he'd look hot in anything. Or nothing. "I couldn't care less either."

3

BINOCULARS AROUND his neck, Carr leaned against the aft railing and stared at the moonlit water where his boat bobbed at the dock.

At nearly eleven o'clock on a Wednesday, the bar was the only place that was hopping. Jack's boat was still out, so it seemed the only thing to do was wait.

His thoughts returned, as they had a million times, to the night before and the kiss he'd shared with Malina Blair. Of course, describing what they'd shared as a mere kiss diminished the encounter by miles.

Touching her had been like holding lightning in his bare hands.

She—

He halted his thoughts as he sensed movement behind him on the dock. He didn't flinch or turn, but his heart rate picked up speed.

Were Jack's buddies back?

He hadn't seen them since that night he'd found the coffee grounds nearly three weeks ago.

Were more drugs being delivered? Were there even drugs involved at all? Something odd was certainly going on, but had he jumped to conclusions based on the coffee grounds? Malina had passed off the connection between drugs and coffee. Was she right, or was she simply trying to demonstrate that he had no business messing around in her case?

If these guys were drug dealers, they were certainly ruthless. And while he could hold his own in a courtroom, he acknowledged for a stark moment that he might just be out of his element in this particular world.

He could battle, but he wasn't trained in any physical combat beyond the conniving elegance of the fencing ring. Brutality wasn't part of his life. And, candidly, he was more brains than brawn.

As he heard a click on the starboard side of the boat, he spun on the balls of his feet and crouched at the same time.

"Smooth," said a familiar voice. "But I still wouldn't have missed."

The next second, a powerful flashlight blinded him. Cursing, he rose and held his hands in front of his face. Malina Blair's shadow was barely discernible. "Is that really necessary?"

The light flicked off.

He blinked and saw spots as his eyes adjusted back to the darkness. Before he'd fully recovered, she was inches from him.

She tapped the binoculars. "A little late for bird-watching."

Dressed in black, her arm was a shadow that ended in a lethal-looking gun pointed to the sky. With her dark hair pulled back tightly from her face, the first thing he could see clearly was her startlingly turquoise eyes. He had the crazy, poetic urge to drown himself in them.

"Just what the hell do you think you're doing?" she asked, narrowing those eyes as she holstered her pistol.

He wanted to see her hair loose and tangled around her beautiful face. He wanted to feel the strands brush across his bare skin. He wanted to bury his body in her softness and hear her breath catch as she lost herself in the pleasure of his touch.

"Contemplating a late-night cruise," he managed to return finally.

She shook her head in disbelief.

If he admitted the truth—that he was imagining her in his bed—would she shoot him or throw him overboard?

Or would she respond as she had the night before? With need and heat and a longing for even more?

She poked her finger in his chest, backing him against the railing. "I thought I made it clear that you should keep your distance from this case."

"Did you?" He angled his head and gave her a smile that she clearly wasn't buying. "I recall that conversation a bit differently. I remember saying I understood what you thought my involvement in the case should be." He paused significantly. "I never agreed to the terms."

She paced away, then back. "Why do you think lawyers get a bad rap when it comes to honesty?"

"Because honesty and truth are two entirely different concepts. Do you have on black underwear, too?" When she glared at him, he shrugged. "I've always wondered about the wardrobe for the undercover espionage thing."

She stopped pacing. Her fists were clenched by her sides, and he decided he enjoyed needling her almost as much as he enjoyed touching her. "How about you leave the espionage to James Bond and me to handle this case?"

"Sorry, my investment in the outcome is too great."

"What investment?"

He made a sweeping gesture to the area around him. "My island, remember?" *Among other beautiful things I want to hold close.* "I need to see this through."

"And I said I'd consult you. The stakeouts you need to leave to me."

He raised his eyebrows. "Stakeout? I'm just enjoying the night air."

With a huff that was utterly female and so unlike her, Malina leaned back against the railing next to him. "How are honesty and truth different?"

"Honesty refers to integrity, candor. Truth is answering a question without lying."

She cast him a surprised glance. "That's a despicable distinction."

He nodded, and the barb of criticism hit in ways she couldn't imagine, even though he knew she'd read his case files. "It's the law."

"According to whom?"

"Anybody who's called upon to defend themselves or someone else in court."

"Someone guilty?"

The barb turned poisonous, spreading through him like cancer. "Everyone's entitled to a defense—even the supposed guilty."

"Is that how you sleep at night?"

With fury burning inside him, he faced her, crossing his arms over his chest. The fact that part of his anger stemmed from embarrassment only fueled his indignation. "Do you want to debate legal procedures? How about the merits of tort reform?" He nodded toward her holstered pistol. "As good as you might be with that, I'm better at the law, so don't even think about screwing with me on that subject.

"A lawyer presents his or her case. A judge or jury determines guilt or the level of judgment. That's it. That's the system where we all work." He leaned into her. "If, however, you want to screw me in other ways, I'm more than happy to oblige."

Her eyes narrowed as she stared at him. And either his *honesty* or his crudeness had finally shocked her into silence.

Unable to face her or himself, he stormed across the deck and down into the cabin. He slammed the door behind him, then tore the binoculars from around his neck and flung them and himself onto the couch. Through the window above him the moon cast its haunting light.

Several moments later, the cabin door opened.

"I'm sorry I took my frustration out on you," she said, flopping against the wall opposite him and crossing her arms over her chest.

For some reason, her frustration calmed him instantly. "I'm sorry I did the same. Why are you so annoyed?"

"I didn't get much sleep last night."

"Why not?"

"The case. Concern for my job."

"No other reason?"

She moved toward him. His heart jumped.

When she stopped beside the sofa, so close their legs nearly touched, he felt the heat pumping off her, as well as a seductive scent, which could have been perfume or simply the innate lure of her skin. Both twined their way around his senses.

"You," she said. "I thought about you."

Though her tone was an accusation, he wasn't offended. She'd thrown his world off balance. Now he knew he'd done the same for her.

He also knew he should stand, but he wasn't sure his legs would hold him.

She skimmed her fingertips across his shoulder. "What've you done to me?"

Part of him wanted to tell her to run. He wasn't worthy of her time or attention. But he wasn't capable of that kind of nobility.

He captured her hand in his and kissed the underside of her wrist, where her pulse beat strong and thick. "In an effort to be truly honest, I should admit I was enjoying the night air and hoping you'd show up for a stakeout."

She slid down onto the sofa beside him. "And I knew you wouldn't give up your involvement in this case."

"Are we pursuing the case because we want to solve it, or are we pursuing it to have an excuse to be together?"

"I'm not sure."

"Does it matter which is true?"

"Honestly?" She smiled, leaning toward him, her lips an inch from his. "No."

Her tongue teased his bottom lip, then her teeth nipped the same spot. He hardened in an instant.

With a tug of her wrist, he pulled her against him, crushing her against his chest, relishing the way her heart hammered against him, as if trying to escape and join his. Angling her head, she deepened the kiss and wrapped her arms around his neck.

He breathed in the scent of clean cotton and, if he wasn't mistaken, gun oil.

She was a combination of tenderness and teeth that he found intriguing, stimulating and irresistible.

His erection throbbed. His ears buzzed.

The gentle rocking of the boat beneath them belied the electricity in the air. In the dark, shadows mingled. Hot breath and seeking hands sparked passion. Forgetting who she was and her real purpose in his life, he surrendered to the moment as he hadn't in a very long time.

But before he'd taken his next breath, she had her pistol drawn and her back plastered against the wall next to the cabin's exterior door. "Get down," she whispered.

His hands tingled. He still had the scent of her clinging to him. "I—"

"That buzzing in your ears isn't my substantial powers of seduction. It's a boat motor."

"How do you know my ears are buzzing?"

"Because mine are, too. *Get down*."

He slid from the sofa onto the floor and watched her peek between the blinds on the glass door. With a great deal of effort, he could now separate the humming in his ears from the motor outside.

She was cool, calm and in charge. He was a quivering mass of need. There was a serious balance issue with this relationship already. If there even was a relationship, which he wasn't sure about. They'd only been introduced two days ago. Didn't these things take time to develop? Didn't the fact that she was in his life only to solve a case make anything meaningful impractical? And hadn't he decided he was through with anything that didn't have meaning?

Then again, her ears were buzzing, too.

Eschewing dignity, he crawled across the cabin, then

rose beside Malina. "There are times when I feel like a freshman in the throes of my first crush."

"The throes of—" She stopped, turning her head to glare at him. "Don't throw. Don't crush. Be still."

She looked lean and sexy, her pistol raised beside her and pointing at the ceiling. Her expression was focused, her body braced. Desire tightened his stomach. "Is that thing loaded?"

She peeked between the blinds again. "Do you ever shut up?"

He pressed his lips to the shell of her ear. "If you keep my mouth occupied in some other way."

She ignored the invitation and said, "I think it's your buddy Jack."

"So we work now and play later?"

"I'm always working."

She used the tip of her gun to move the blinds aside, and he watched over her shoulder as Jack's boat puttered past and turned into its slip. "That's him, right?" she asked in a hoarse whisper.

"That's the boat."

She snorted. "You're such a lawyer."

"Unless there's now a rash of boat thieves running over the island intent on disrupting the general well-being of the citizenry, I assume Jack's the pilot."

"Hell. A wordy lawyer."

"I'm well paid for each and every syllable."

"Do you ever feel guilty for making that money on the tide of pain and suffering your clients have to weather?"

Something ugly clenched inside him. "All the time," he said lightly.

Part of the tension he felt must have slipped through

his tone, because she glanced at him. "Cheap shot. Sorry."

"I'm used to it."

"So I'm all the more sorry."

"I appreciate the—"

"Hold on. He's moving."

And Jack was.

He emerged from the cabin with a small box tucked beneath his arm. The box appeared to be made of ordinary, brown cardboard. It measured no more than half a foot wide and long. Jack was whistling as he stepped off his boat and onto the dock.

For some reason, the upbeat tune made Carr's blood boil. "Let's follow him."

Malina planted her hand in the center of his chest. "Let's watch."

After a few moments, Jack disappeared up the stairs toward the marina bar—and no doubt the parking lot beyond.

"We should go after him."

"I will. I know where he lives." Tucking her pistol back into its holster, Malina opened the door and stepped out. "Let's look around a little first."

As they moved slowly along the dock, Carr studied the bobbing *American Dream*. Something was fishy about Jack's boat—and it didn't have anything to do with nets or rods. "I don't suppose you could turn your head while I pop the cabin lock and see what old Jack had hidden beneath his mattress?"

"Not yet."

Though Malina's back was to him, Carr raised his eyebrows. "So you're not saying no? How liberal of you, Agent—"

"Hang on."

As Malina bent to one knee, Carr moved closer to her. More coffee maybe? If so, Jack really ought to find a sealed box to carry his illicit merchandise in. Didn't the man know about plastic containers? They even had fresh seal plastic bags now. Double-zippered to ensure the contents stayed tightly enclosed.

"Well, now," Malina said in a low, excited tone that immediately captured his attention. "It seems your neighbor does have a side business, though I'm not sure how drugs, art or coffee enters into it."

Carr moved his attention to her clenched fist, which she held out in front of her. "How so?"

"It appears Mr. Rafton went for the sparkle instead."

When she opened her hand, sitting on a scrap of white cloth, a large, loose diamond glittered back at him from her steady palm.

4

RISING, Malina studied the stone in her hand. Four, maybe five carats. But the thrill of discovery was rapidly being overcome by questions with no answers.

Hamilton, standing so close she felt completely wrapped in his enticing, somewhat old-fashioned sandalwood scent, seemed to realize this as well. "You make people think you're smuggling drugs, when you're really smuggling diamonds? That seems…"

"Stupid."

"And what about the artwork?" Hamilton asked. "I've bought enough paintings to recognize the crates in which they're shipped."

"Decoys? Or he's into more than gems."

"Coffee grounds and painting crates to disguise diamonds?"

Malina shrugged. "Gold and jewels are a big commodity now. With the stock market and economy shaky, tangible assets are hot. Banks, museums and collectors are being hit left and right. Smuggling stolen goods is in vogue once again."

"But Jack—head of a smuggling operation?" Hamilton

frowned. "He doesn't have the nerve or the brains. He's a nice, average guy."

"And yet he's already managed to stir up a lot of red tape. Paintings and diamonds are major theft—FBI jurisdiction, in other words. Drugs are DEA. Plus, there's local law enforcement to coordinate and possibly the Coast Guard if any of us needed to board his boat in open water. Maybe this is a more complex operation than it seems."

Hamilton shook his head. "Sorry. I can't give Jack that kind of credit." When her gaze flicked to his, he amended, "Bad guy credit, of course. He's just not that creative a thinker, not devious enough."

"Maybe you're the one who's not devious enough."

"Oh, no. I am."

How did she respond to that? His odd, self-deprecating humor had a darker source, she was sure. Were all those profitable lawsuits becoming mundane?

She knew he'd left his practice in New York City two years ago to settle on Palmer's Island, where he'd volunteered to be the unpaid staff lawyer to a variety of charities and churches. Up until they'd met, she'd been certain he was behind the scenes building a big case—tort reform be damned—that would bust out on the national scene, sending him around the talk shows and law conferences for some time to come.

But that cold-blooded plan didn't mesh with the man she'd met—and kissed.

I like to walk on the beach.

She believed those words more than she trusted the evidence she'd seen in her background check.

How far the mighty had fallen indeed.

"You observed Jack taking a payoff," she said, to get her focus back on the case as she folded the cloth carefully around the diamond and tucked it in her pants pocket. "He could be a middleman with someone more creative pulling the strings."

"True."

"Who would have the nerves and the brains around here to smuggle diamonds?"

"I can find out." A smile stretched across his gorgeous face. "In fact, we both can."

"Why am I not surprised?" Malina crossed her arms over her chest. "I should be ordering you back to your office and out of my business."

He slid his fingers down her sweater-covered arm, barely touching but easily reminding her of the intimacies they'd already shared. And the ones likely to come. Need shimmered between them like the glow of the moon overhead. "But you won't."

"No."

"Because you know I won't listen, or because you know you can use me to solve the case?"

"Both. I assume you already have an idea for finding out about the smuggling?"

"You know me well."

"You constantly think several steps ahead." She shrugged. "It's a trait I recognize."

He angled his head. "I imagine so. I've been invited to a yacht party on Friday night. All the island's elite crowd will be there, including Jack."

"How do you know he'll come?"

"I'll dangle the opportunity to mix with rich potential clients. He'll be there. And since the host is new around the island, and this recent criminal activity is new, I wonder if the two connect?"

"So Rafton and this guy don't already know each other?"

"Maybe. It'll be interesting to observe them and find out. You can go as my date."

The word *date* made her frown. "So we go under-cover?"

The sensually wicked grin that never failed to make her pulse pound teased his lips. "Absolutely."

"Just remember I'm in charge."

"How could I forget?" When she flicked him a suspicious glance, he added, "You are armed, after all."

So are you, she longed to add. That smile should be registered as a lethal weapon.

"I need to get going," she said, and even she recognized the regret in her tone.

His hand cupped her jaw gently. "I was hoping you'd stay awhile."

"I have evidence to log, and I need to do some background work on the party and the guests. Can you get me the information?"

Surprisingly, he didn't press her to stay. "I'll send it over by the morning."

Why was she disappointed he'd given over to the demands of the case so easily? Why was there a part of her that wanted him to press her into staying? Into going back to his boat and finishing what they'd started?

Deliberately, she shook the idea from her mind. "Who's the sheriff on the island?"

"Tyler Landry. Former Marine. He's just been on the job a few months, but he's sharp."

"At some point I'll need to inform him about at least some of what I'm doing, what I suspect."

"Federal cooperation with the locals?" Hamilton paused, amusement tugging his lips. "How progressive of you."

"I can be reasonable…eventually. But I want to keep

this party business quiet, see what happens. I'm telling nobody but the SAC. Even though I've got probable cause for a search warrant on the boat, I'm not going to ask for it." She smiled fiercely. "I'm also not calling the DEA. This is all mine—for now."

"Ours. And you might consider bringing in Landry sooner rather than later. You'll get his support and discretion."

"You know him well."

"He's married to a good friend of mine, and they happen to be my neighbors."

"I'll think about it."

This case was pretty personal all around—not that she should be surprised on an island of this size.

She certainly hadn't anticipated being involved, though.

And, like it or not, she was involved.

Getting personally mixed up with a witness was a risky career move, but at some point during the night she'd quit pretending she could resist Carr Hamilton's allure. As long as they kept their relationship quiet and separate from the case, and as long as she reminded herself that he was simply a pleasurable means to an end, there was no reason she couldn't be a normal woman and enjoy herself.

Sex was a great stress buster, and she rarely took the time and effort to indulge in personal needs. Especially since her *last* risky career move.

She sighed.

Then again, maybe *risky* was a colossal understatement.

HE WANTED HER too much.

As Carr watched Malina walk down the pier away from him, he fought to ignore the aching need in his body.

It was better to let her go for now. He needed to re-group, and she was wise in using caution at them being seen together.

But it was hard.

Hell, *he* was hard. Perpetually, it seemed.

With no carnal relief in sight and troubled by the intensity of his attraction, he resisted the urge to slip into Jack's cabin to do a little off-the-record searching and instead headed to his own slip. He locked up and checked the dock ties before casually making his way to The Heron. There, he drank a whiskey and chatted with Jimmy, communicating to all that he was just a regular guy going about his regular routine.

Certainly not spying on a fellow islander or planning an undercover yacht party operation with the FBI.

All the while he talked and drank, however, he couldn't get Malina Blair's pillow-soft lips and vivid eyes out of his mind.

As he'd traveled his new path of redemption, he'd begun to long for a woman to share his life with. Some-one who might not necessarily have to know the man he used to be, but could appreciate the man he was trying to become.

Unfortunately, the one he wanted had instigated a deep background check on him and probably knew all his dirty secrets. One who was bound by regulations to keep her distance, as well as harboring a deep longing to escape from the island that had become his saving grace.

There was irony in that realization, as well as a hint of divine punishment.

Of course that didn't mean he wouldn't fight to make her crave him as much as he did her. Or strive to change her mind about both him and his island home. Or do his absolute best to circumvent, dodge or outwit rules and retribution, no matter how much they were needed and deserved.

Most would say the gray areas were where he did his best work anyway.

THOUGH CARR HAD spoken to Malina a few times by phone over the past two days, he hadn't seen her, and he found himself pacing his front parlor as he awaited her arrival on Friday afternoon.

The warm and sunny March day had inspired him to open his windows, so the scent of salt and sea flowed through the house. He'd called his cleaning service and had them come out that morning to polish the considerable amount of stainless steel and glass.

In a rare show of indecisiveness, he'd changed clothes three times before deciding on a pair of crisply pressed navy pants and a white oxford-cloth shirt.

His heart leaped as the doorbell rang, and he had to force himself to take a deep breath and roll his shoulders before closing the few feet between him and the door.

A curvy blonde, wearing a short, formfitting, royal-purple halter-top dress and gold stilettos, stood on his porch. For one jarring moment he thought a new form of door-to-door sales was being launched—and a very enticing one at that.

Only the tough glare in the woman's turquoise eyes gave away her identity.

"I spent two hours messing with this getup, so don't even think about critiquing."

Somehow, Carr managed to speak around his swollen tongue. "Wouldn't dream of it."

He stepped back and extended his arm to invite her in, then, groaning, watched her walk past him. Her long, toned, tanned legs had his blood running hot and his palms sweating.

He was supposed to *pretend* to be crazy about her all night?

Gee, that would be difficult.

Following her, he commented, "Why, Agent Blair, what lovely legs you have."

She cast him an amused look over her shoulder. "Cute. You look like the typical yacht-going millionaire. Where's your watch cap?"

"At the cleaners. I didn't expect you to appear incognito."

"We agreed to do this undercover, right?"

Heroically, he resisted the urge to point out that his best undercover work didn't require any clothes at all.

Especially since he'd rather demonstrate than chatter needlessly.

"We did agree," he said. "Well, given your usual choice of binding your hair back and wearing either unobtrusive navy or black, I doubt anybody would recognize you in *that*."

She glanced down at herself and shrugged. "I can't take the chance. I've interviewed several people on the island regarding Jack Rafton." She continued to walk down the hall. "Plus, the mayor's on the guest list. I met him at an event in Charleston, so he knows I'm an agent."

"I should have considered that."

"I did. It's my—" She stopped, her head twisting to scan the area around her.

The entire back half of the house where she now stood was curved in two places like towers and made up mostly of windows to take advantage of the point's majestic view. One tower even held a curved steel staircase that twined its way up three floors to a small observation deck overlooking the rippling ocean.

He watched her turn and take in the steel railing bracketing the wide, floating staircase that dominated the two-story living and kitchen areas and led to the balcony walkway and upstairs bedrooms. Her gaze flicked over the black marble countertops, the glass and stainless-steel tables, the art on the walls, the sculptures, the white decor and furniture mixed with bare splashes of red and blue.

It was quite a contrast to his conservative and comforting, antique-heavy office.

"My job," she finished finally, her gaze finding his and holding. "Do you like surprising people?"

"Do you often put on a short skirt and heels, let the bad guys take a good, long look at those fabulous legs and initiate a sting under the insignia of justice?"

She narrowed her eyes. "I try to keep the sluttiness down to once a week."

"What a shame."

"Did you design and build this house?" she asked, ignoring his come-on.

"Yes."

"So who decorated your office?"

"I did."

"Huh."

Clearly, he'd stumped her. He liked the idea. He also couldn't help his gaze dropping to her supremely impressive cleavage. "Where do you carry your gun in an outfit like that?"

"Wouldn't you like to know."

He grinned. "Definitely. Come on, where?"

"I don't. And trust me I'm not happy about it."

He closed the distance between them, bracing his

hands at her narrow waist. "You're unarmed?" he clarified, dipping his head to brush his lips across her cheek.

"I didn't say that."

"Okay." Of course now that he was touching her, breathing in a warm, floral scent that was a departure from her usual clean cotton, he couldn't care less about weapons.

"I have a switchblade strapped to my thigh," she finished.

He pressed his lips to her earlobe. "Maybe I should check to be sure it's loaded properly."

She swatted his shoulder in a totally uncharacteristic playful gesture, then stepped back. "You keep your distance."

He tried to look insulted. "I thought you were my blonde bimbo, and I was your morally ambiguous sugar daddy."

"You have quite an imagination. And you need to remember this is my op. You're the reluctant ally I'm using to close this case and get my career back on track."

Leaning back, he tried to look comically insulted, even though his gut clenched. "Being morally ambiguous, I can accept that."

She turned away. "We should get going."

"You don't want a tour?"

She cast one last and—if he wasn't mistaken—longing look around the living room, her gaze lingering on the staircase to the observation deck. "Maybe some other time."

As they headed outside, she moved toward her government-issue sedan, paused, then swore.

Since Carr could all but hear the silent argument in her head, he said nothing. He simply paused beside the garage doors. Being so close to the ocean, the house was raised above the ground and the lower level was all storage. In his case, the garage held his golf clubs, yard tools, pool and hot tub chemicals and his Triumph Spitfire.

Finally, Malina turned. "I guess we should take your car."

He pressed his lips together briefly. "If you insist…"

He pressed a button on the remote keychain in his pocket, and the garage doors slid open. After assisting blonde-but-still-stunning Malina into the passenger seat, he pulled away from the house—with the top down, naturally.

"Will the breeze upset your wig, or did you dye your hair?"

Her eyes popped wide. "Dye my—" She stopped, and her jaw tightened. "I'm not vain. I just wouldn't dye my hair for an op." She paused. "Probably. It's a wig, if you have to know. It's on, and it's not going anywhere."

"Good." He paused as he pulled out on Beach Road. "I like your hair as it is. Very Thai."

"I'm an American, like you."

"And while there's a remnant of the Scots in me, there's a world of Polynesian in you. It isn't an insult, you know. The beauty of your ancestors is renowned, and despite the chaotic mix of many island nations, differing religions and backgrounds, plus the selling of rum-infused umbrella drinks in coconuts, your culture has even miraculously survived the formidable tourist industry."

She looked over at him. "Is that your wordy way of telling me I'm pretty just the way I am?"

He chuckled. "It is."

"Thanks, but I really need to focus on this op."

"Sorry." He fought to hide his disappointment. "Just trying to stay in character."

She slid her hand across his thigh so suddenly he jolted. "I have to keep my professional life away from my personal life. When I let my emotions get mixed up with my job, I run into trouble. You know why I was sent here, so you understand."

His jaw tightened, but he nodded. Damned if he'd let her past—in which she'd done nothing wrong, by the way—dictate the need crawling through his veins. And she wanted him, too. If she didn't, he'd bow out. He'd help close the case, then move on without a word of regret. What did he have to do to—

"Whatever happens between us has to stay private and after hours."

Interrupted from his private rant, he glanced at her. "So you acknowledge there is something between us."

A rare smile bloomed on her face. "Oh, yeah."

He momentarily forgot how to shift gears. "So, after hours...when are those exactly?"

"My work is my life. I don't have hours. But I think I can fit you in somewhere."

Before he could be insulted at being "fit in" between suspects and reports, she leaned over, scraping her lips across his jaw. "This party has to end sometime, right?"

Talk about surprise.

As abruptly as the sensuous woman buried inside her had appeared, Malina leaned back in her seat, her eyes all business. "I followed up on your monthly garage tip and found Rafton's Lotus. It's shiny and obvious. I also found the record of the purchase."

"You traced it all the way back under the name John Smith? Must have been some search."

She snorted in derision. "Not that hard. You were right about his lack of creativity, and there haven't been that many domestic sales of the Lotus in the last several months. Especially not ones with Charleston as the delivery point."

Carr braked hard. "He had it shipped to Charleston?"

"Atlanta would have been wiser. L.A. or New York would have been seriously smart. But, just as you pointed out, he's not exactly a master criminal. You know how many Ardent Red Lotus Elises are registered in South Carolina?"

"Not many."

"One."

Despite his dedication to stopping whatever Jack was doing, Carr winced. Would he, even in his most morally ambiguous days, have had a defense for that purchase?

Unfortunately, yes.

"Something's certainly up with Rafton," Malina mused. "Whether he's simply a lousy money manager or a thief and/or smuggler..." She shrugged. "It's too soon to tell. What about the Kendricks? Do you know them? He has a note in our files, due to the unsolved murder of his parents."

"Aidan and Sloan. Her father was the sheriff for many years. He just retired in January, and Aidan is a successful businessman many times over. They're good friends of mine."

At her questioning glance, he added, "Yes, I know everyone on the island—the advantages of living in a small town. Despite my scheming, money-grubbing ways, even Sister Mary Katherine and I have bonded."

Malina raised her eyebrows. "Sister? As in Catholic nun?"

"She makes all the lawyers meet bimonthly."

"Wise lady."

"She certainly is." And a forgiving one, as well. She'd assured him even the worst of society had a place in heaven, should they strive to find their way. "You two are a lot alike."

"I doubt that."

"No, you are." And the more he compared the two women, the more he was convinced. "You both have a titanium center of strength. You stand on the side of what's right, no matter the risk. You're both stubborn and sure your way is the only way."

"That last part sounds just like me."

"Fortunately for both of you, I'm around to keep everyone flexible and on their toes."

Malina flicked him a surprised look. "You mean you spend all the time you're not butting into my case, following around a Catholic nun and telling her how to do her job?"

Saying nothing, Carr pulled into the yacht club parking lot. Finally, as he maneuvered the Spitfire into a space, he commented, "With conversations like this burned into my memory, is it any wonder I'm constantly trying to get you into my bed?"

"I thought my sarcasm would discourage you."

"It makes me want to shut you up by kissing you until you forget what you were talking about in the first place." He turned, bracing his arm across the back of her seat. "In fact, let's practice that technique now."

Before she could respond with more than widened

eyes, he'd captured her mouth with his. He slid his tongue into her mouth, seducing her with his touch, since his words often seemed to have an unpredictable effect. Though he'd always been enticed by her simple scent, he had to admit the warm spice radiating from her golden skin suited her, or at least suited Malina, if not necessarily Agent Blair.

The contrast between moments when she willingly gave herself over to her needs and her absolute fierceness always delighted him. Layers and layers of heat lingered beneath her tough exterior, and he couldn't wait to uncover them all.

She laid her hands on his chest, angling her head, giving back as much as he longed to draw from her. Her lips were soft and seeking, and touching her was, as always, amazing.

When they separated, each breathing hard, her pupils were dilated. She curled her fingers into the fabric of his shirt. "What was I saying?" she asked, sounding dazed.

"I recall a long discourse on my charm no longer being completely inert."

"Discourse on—" She jerked back, her eyes clearing of desire. "Hang on, didn't we agree to keep personal and professional moments separate?"

"Actually, we didn't. You requested that personal moments between us be kept private and after hours. I will agree that's wise. However, since you're currently wearing a disguise and preparing to interrogate and spy on any number of mostly law-abiding citizens for the next few hours, I figured this could actually be classified as a professional fondling." He smoothed a strand of blond hair off her cheek. "We do have our roles to play, don't we?"

Her eyes sparked with temper. "We're going to talk about the rules of engagement later, Counselor. Got it?"

"Should I put down that appointment in my after-hours calendar?"

"I'll check the ammunition in my Glock and get back to you."

Smiling, Carr opened his door. As he stood, he noticed Jack helping a buxom redhead from his car a few spaces away.

Let the war games begin.

5

"WE'RE SO HAPPY you chose our humble island to visit," Mayor Harvey Kelso said with a self-important smile belying his words.

Malina sipped from her champagne glass and tried to infuse enthusiasm into her tone. "It's such a lovely spot."

"Made all the more lovely by your presence."

Malina drank more champagne.

At this rate, she was going to be either pissed and drunk or drunk and fired when she strangled the idiotic, golf-obsessed mayor of this crappy little island she'd landed on.

"We strive to cater to both young professionals as well as families here on Palmer's Island," the mayor continued. "We're also working to attract a premier golf tournament. Unfortunately, our single course is only nine holes, so the PGA won't take us seriously. We're landlocked, and the historical society refuses to budge on their properties. Do they expect us to build greens in the Atlantic?" Shaking his head at this injustice, he smiled nevertheless. "I'm sure the tourism council would love to hear about your vacation priorities."

At least he wasn't hitting on her. Since she knew the mayor had been married for more than a decade and had four kids, she could find some comfort in the realization that he was only interested in her disposable vacation income, not her cleavage.

Still, finding out the mayor was an egomaniac but not a cheat was hardly her priority for this particular operation.

Her partner had abandoned her twenty minutes ago—leaving her safely in the mayor's company as he went off in search of Jack and the yacht's owner—the actual suspects in this little drama, the ones *she* was supposed to be observing. In return, she was beginning to wonder about the suicide rate of intelligent blondes with big boobs.

"Harvey, don't upset the new people," a smooth, unfamiliar male voice interjected. "It disturbs the tax base."

Malina looked over her shoulder to see a dark-haired man and a blonde woman. They were a beautiful couple—lovely features, lightly tanned skin, dressed beach casual and connected by more than just their entwined hands.

"Not to mention the greens fees," the mayor said, lifting his whiskey glass to the newcomers. "Have you met Sandy?"

The man extended his hand. "No, but Carr told us he'd found a gem." Shaking Malina's hand, his silver eyes gleamed. "I'm Aidan Kendrick. My wife, Sloan." He urged the woman at his side into the circle.

Sloan gave Malina a brief greeting, then a discreet sweep from head to toe, her gaze alert and curious.

"Nice to meet you both," Malina said, realizing these were the friends Hamilton had mentioned and that he'd most likely told them her true identity. She wasn't sure, however, how wise that decision was. Generally, the fewer people involved in an undercover op, the better.

Especially untrained civilians.

Dear heaven, the future of her career might hang in the balance of a nosy lawyer, a semiretired business-man, the former sheriff's daughter, who was a librarian and president of the historical society, and the general effectiveness of a push-up bra.

Before she could contemplate how she'd allowed her-self to fall into that professional pitfall, the mayor spoke. "Aidan, have you given any more thought to investing in those old properties on the north end of the island? We could really use another nine holes. We should be able to compete with Kiawah."

"We're not a resort community," Sloan said, shifting her attention to the mayor and narrowing her eyes in the process. "We have plenty of those around. And we're not interested in tearing down a seventeenth-century church to make way for a damn putting green."

Harvey lost his ingratiating politician's smile in the space of a heartbeat. "You and the historical society are always looking for a way to attract more tourists. I just don't see why we can't do that with the golfers, too. They spend plenty of money in our shops and restaurants."

"And we're grateful," Sloan returned. "But we're not destroying the history and natural beauty of this island for ready cash."

The same debate had played out for decades on Ma-lina's home island of Kauai. They needed tourists for economic survival, and, actually, most locals liked shar-ing the pride and beauty of their home. But there was the danger of going too far. Of strip malls, T-shirt shops and theme restaurants overwhelming the environment to the point of destruction.

"Regardless," Aidan said, "I was outbid on the northern properties."

Sloan scowled. "And, trust me, I'm not happy about that either."

Surprise, then speculation crossed the mayor's face. "Really? By who?"

"Our host," Aidan said.

Malina jerked her attention from Aidan's handsome features back to her job. "Why do you think he was so determined to get the properties?"

The mayor glanced at her. "You're interested in real estate, Sandy? I thought Carr said you were a model."

Malina clenched her teeth. *Of course he did.* Was her career worth this? "I won't always be twenty-three and perfect." Following this self-aggrandized announcement, she giggled.

Sloan pressed her lips together as if suppressing a smirk.

Aidan nodded sagely. "Sadly, Harvey, it's true. Diversification is essential to any portfolio."

It was no wonder Hamilton and this guy were friends. Both were slick as the ice this island might see every millennium or so.

Before Malina could probe Aidan Kendrick further about the properties, a tall, silver-haired man in an expensive-looking navy suit approached their group. Their host, Simon Ellerby, as Malina knew from the pictures she'd found during her research. "Beautiful women who laugh are always welcome at my parties," he said, his gaze locked on Malina's. "Do you mind if I join you?"

He had an exotic accent that was faintly, but vaguely, European. He was tan and handsome—which seemed to be a common trait with nearly everyone on the island— and wore a diamond pinky ring on his left hand.

As Aidan introduced him to Malina—or, more accurately, to Sandy—she watched him for any false notes in the wealthy boat captain persona. She found none. Yet the perfection itself was a fault. He seemed to be playing a part, like an actor in a play.

The FBI had suspiciously little information on the man, who claimed to be nearly fifty, and Malina sensed she wouldn't have much more luck this afternoon.

"I was telling everyone about the properties you bought on the north end of the island," Aidan said. "Do you have any firm plans for them?"

"Renovation probably," Ellerby said. "The smaller houses could be sold as is or divided into rental duplexes, and the big house could be a B and B, or maybe apartments."

The mayor frowned. "How do you feel about golf?"

"The big house was built in 1867," Sloan said after a swift glare in the mayor's direction. "It would be nice to keep the original structure intact."

Ellerby angled his head. "Was it really? My lawyer handled the transaction, so I haven't seen many of the details."

Malina widened her eyes and tried to look both confused and impressed. "You bought a house you haven't even seen?"

Ellerby laughed indulgently. "I do that quite often." He swept his hand around to indicate the deck where they were standing. "I bought *Le Bijou* here sight unseen on the recommendation of a colleague. A mere whim."

"What does Le Bee—" Malina broke off, her face flushing. "Is that French for something?"

"It is indeed." His eyes gleamed, hard as the translation she knew he was about to reveal. *"The Jewel."*

"An expensive whim, Simon," Sloan said. "The historical society would love to have your support at our next fundraiser."

"Of course, of course," Ellerby said lightly. "With such a lovely invitation, and from the president herself, how could I resist?"

"Be careful what you promise," Hamilton said as he approached. "Sloan is a shark when it comes to the society." He slid his arm around Malina's waist, and she immediately felt the spark of desire that always accompanied his presence.

It was distracting and, for a moment, she simply absorbed his elegance, the enticing scent that clung to his skin and clothes.

"Hey, all," Jack Rafton said as he and his redhead date walked up, bringing Malina's thoughts back to her job. He toasted the host with a crystal tumbler. "Great party."

Ellerby nodded graciously. "Thank you. Carr tells me you're in insurance."

"I am. Auto, home, life—the whole deal." He smiled with the winning charm of a practiced salesperson. "I handle most of the boats in the area, too."

"I've seen you around the marina a few times. I assume you keep close tabs on your clients."

"Naturally. I also have my own Sea Ray in slip twenty-three."

Without seeming to, Malina watched their exchange

closely. While Simon Ellerby seemed relaxed, she observed Rafton taking frequent sips from his drink. His gaze skipped from the group around him, to the deck beneath his feet, then the clouds in the distance.

Carr, she noticed, was left to listen to Rafton's date ramble on about the lack of decent nightclubs on Palmer's Island. Poor man.

The conversation moved on around her, and she prodded with questions from time to time that she hoped would help her get a measure of their suspects. But she was constantly aware of her partner, her witness, her would-be lover…whatever he was besides gorgeous, tempting…irresistible.

Part of her couldn't believe she was distracted during an op, and part of her was fascinated that a romantic interest could bring about such a change.

Her career was her life. No one and nothing had ever swayed her from that path.

Why now? Why Hamilton? She had no idea.

With her own motives and actions so cloudy, she decided to pursue someone else's. Wasn't it wiser, easier, to focus on others and not look too deeply inside herself?

"Why *The Jewel?*" she asked Ellerby.

He smiled, though no genuine emotion reached his cold gray eyes. "Isn't it obvious? I love being surrounded by beautiful things."

LATER, as the sun set, casting a torrid mix of orange and red light across the sky and churning sea, Carr found himself alone with Malina at the yacht's aft. The propeller churned the water into mountains of white foam.

It was a night for gazing at the moon, long kisses and breathy sighs.

Somehow, though, he didn't think the woman beside him—even in disguise—was planning that sort of evening.

"Sandy?" she asked, her tone clearly annoyed.

"Well," he began, leaning against the railing and relishing the illumination of her profile in the fading light of the sun, "the name had to fit with your character. Blonde, somewhat ditzy bikini model…Sandy seemed to fit." He angled his head. "The stereotype might annoy astronauts, doctors and nuclear physicists named Sandy, but remember I was under a considerable time constraint."

"I'm sorry I asked," Malina muttered.

"You played your part well."

"It was physically painful. Is every curvy blonde on the planet subjected to people who talk to them as if they're five years old?"

"I wouldn't know. What did you think of Ellerby?"

"Smooth." She glanced at him. "Not as smooth as you or your buddy Aidan Kendrick, of course, but good enough." Her eyes fired, throwing off the veil of her disguise despite her tight dress and golden hair. "And whim, my ass. He bought this boat for a reason. He does nothing without considering every angle, every possibility very, very carefully."

"I agree."

"And he and Rafton are more than fellow boaters who've passed each other on the dock a few times, the way they both claim."

"Yes, they are."

"That redhead Rafton brought is a complete idiot."

"Yes, she is."

"You're awfully agreeable tonight."

He stepped closer, sliding his arms around her waist. "You're incredibly beautiful."

Her gaze flicked to his and held. "Is this part of the op? Or are we after hours now?"

"I think we've worked hard enough for today."

"To serve and protect isn't a normal job."

Coming from anybody else, that sentiment would be corny. But beneath that fierce stare and drive to claw her way up the government ladder of success, Carr knew Malina Blair cared. Certainly about the citizens around her and maybe even about him.

"Serve me," he whispered, pressing his lips against the side of her neck. "And I'll serve you." He could feel her heartbeat accelerate as he moved his hands down her backside, pulling her tight against his body.

"Somebody has to keep their head and do the protecting," she said, though she looped her hands around his neck and pressed her cheek alongside his.

"You can do that again tomorrow." The floral scent of her perfume invaded him as naturally as the sun set on the horizon. His head was swimming and his body aching, and yet he knew he had to tread carefully. Seducing her was like handling unexploded ammunition. Pressing the wrong button could cause them both to implode.

"For now, I'll find somewhere safe and isolated," he said.

She leaned back. "Your boat?"

His heart thumped hard once, then again. He nodded. "Sounds perfect."

"HAMILTON..."

"Right here," Carr said, pausing to give Malina another long kiss as he spun them through the cabin door of his boat. "At your service."

"I'm really not supposed to be doing this," she muttered against his lips, even as she unfastened his belt.

"I won't tell." He grabbed the hem of her dress, tugging it up until it hung around her hips. He slid his palms across her lace-covered butt and closed his eyes as pleasure shot through his body. "I'm very good at keeping secrets."

"I'm not sure I trust you."

Even with her breath hot on his throat, he winced. "The attorney-client relationship is sacred."

"I'm not a client," she returned as she threaded her fingers through his hair, and they moved down the narrow hallway to the bedroom.

"But I've entered into a professional—" he paused to angle her face upward for his kiss "—agreement with you and the FBI to..." He sat on the bed, pulling her between his thighs, closing his eyes as she leaned over him. "To solve this case for the betterment of everyone on Palmer's Island and—"

Her fingers wrapped around his erection and, for once, he lost the power of speech.

With her free hand, she tossed away the blond wig, then ran her fingers through her long, dark hair, scattering pins across the room.

The gesture felt like a sign, the moment of capitulation he'd been waiting for, as if he wasn't sure she'd truly be his beneath the masquerade and restrictions of her job. Her eyes were dark, dark blue and her pupils dilated as she stared at him, clearly enjoying the power she held and yet needy for whatever he desired at the same time.

He caught the edge of her dress and yanked it up and

off her body, then let it drop beside them. A leather strap held a knife sheath to her thigh, making her look like some kind of ancient warrior princess.

He unhooked it himself, his fingers caressing her warm, golden skin before he let that, too, fall to the floor.

She was naked now, except for her lacy panties, and he cupped her breasts like a treasure, gliding his tongue across each distended nipple.

When she moaned softly, exhilaration coursed through him.

Her body was as trimly muscular and amazing as he'd imagined, but more than the physical, he could feel her hunger, her need for fulfillment. Her longing to share both with him and only him. He hoped he wasn't imagining the extra charge through the air, the instinctual chemistry that told him this wasn't casual stress relief or convenient proximity.

Part of him—the part he'd fought to suppress the past several years—reminded him that motivations didn't matter. His need to make reparation for past deeds was being satisfied in many ways, and, after all, desire was desire.

But he'd also learned solitude held no interest.

"You think you could call me by my first name?" he asked as he lay back on the bed, pulling her next to him.

"Maybe…" She flipped open one of his shirt's buttons. He slid his index finger between her legs, beyond the elastic of her panties. "Eventually…" she whispered as her eyes fluttered shut.

While his finger stroked the wet heat between her legs, she squeezed his erection, and he, too, closed his eyes, fighting for control.

The moment she gasped and her thighs clenched, he found a smile. He increased the pressure of his strokes on her sensitive flesh.

Her breathing hitched; her hips rocked.

As her climax burst through her, she let go of him and slumped forward, bracing her hands against the mattress on either side of his head.

The contractions subsiding, she dipped her head and gave him a long, hot, amazing kiss.

"Carr," she said like a litany when they parted.

He smoothed the curtain of her silky hair off her face. "Finally."

Her head cocked, she smiled slightly. "There's more, though, right?"

His erection pulsed. "I certainly hope so."

Leaning back, she straddled his hips and ripped open his shirt, buttons pinging against the walls. The rest of their clothes followed in a flurry of greed and anticipation.

Naked, condom securely in place, Carr rolled on top of her, his hands loving every curve and inch of exposed skin. He fit between her legs, and she wrapped them around him, inviting him into her warmth.

As he surged inside, it seemed he'd waited an eternity to be part of her. Pleasure skated down his spine, even as the urgency to move, to satisfy the clawing need deep in his gut became overwhelming.

Fancy words deserted him. Nothing but the slap of their bodies against each other mattered. Chasing fulfillment. Searching for solace.

Primal, human and instinctive, they knew they had to reach the pinnacle to survive. Maybe tenderness would come later. Maybe not. Their chemistry was as intense as she was distinctly unpredictable.

But as a man who thrived on control, he gloried in losing it when she gripped him hard with her hips, rolled him to his back and let their bodies explode.

MALINA, her body slick with sweat and satisfaction, slid weakly off Carr's body.

Every nerve tingled, vibrated…shimmered. Her skin felt alive as it never had before. She wanted to hold the feelings before they slipped away. For once, she wanted vulnerability and defensiveness to last instead of fighting to banish them, instead of considering them the highest form of weaknesses.

She did trust him, even if she might never be able to tell him.

The gentle rock of the waves beneath the boat lulled her as her eyelids drifted closed, but a nibble on her fingers brought her back to awareness.

Of what she'd done. What she'd risked. What she still longed for.

"Are you still with me?" he asked, his voice husky.

"Barely." She knew she needed to find her clothes and leave. She couldn't seem to come up with a logical reason to move, though her instincts demanded she do so. "I'll come back around," she managed to say as she rolled to her back.

He spooned his body along her side, sliding his thigh over hers, letting his fingers drift up and down her bare stomach.

Shivers raced through her, reigniting desire.

His lips brushed her shoulder. "Soon?"

A smile bloomed from deep within. She looked over at him, into the dark brown of his eyes, letting her gaze drift over the jet-black waves of hair that surrounded his remarkable face. He was beautiful. "You're insatiable," she said instead.

"Is that a crime?"

"I'll check my regulations manual and get back to you."

"I look forward to the consultation."

"That's not going to be now, is it?"

"I'm a lawyer. We get paid to talk. It's instinctive."

"And *that* is the most succinct speech you've ever made."

"You've inspired me."

Something about the tenderness in his tone, which hadn't been there before, put her on edge. "Look, this isn't going to be a thing, right?"

He raised his eyebrows. "A thing?"

She sat up, wishing she could pull a blanket over herself but not wanting him to know she was uncomfortable. "I mean, we're just blowing off steam, aren't we? This case is stressful. You're involved in an atypical situation. It's only natural we'd come together in a way that's more than a professional bond."

"And that's the longest speech I've ever heard you give," he said lightly, though he ceased his rhythmic strokes against her belly. Rising, he snagged his pants from the floor and stepped into them. "Am I correct in assuming you're committed to focusing all your energy on this case?"

What was this about? "You are."

"And aren't you concerned for your job if anyone finds out about us?"

She shrugged. "I guess. But then I don't expect you to go shouting about it all over the island or the Bureau."

"You're taking a risk being with me," he insisted.

Screw being uncomfortable. Now she was pissed, though mostly at herself.

She rolled off the bed and grabbed the first thing she found on the floor—which turned out to be his white dress shirt—and shoved her arms into the sleeves. "Yeah, I suppose I am."

"And your work is your life."

Facing him, she crossed her arms over her chest. "And so?"

"So logic would dictate that I mean something to you beyond someone to casually blow off steam with."

She heard hurt beneath the insult, which was exactly what she didn't want. This was supposed to be simple—chemistry plus hot guy times proximity equals sizzling night. Why was her life so damn complicated these days?

She wanted to run, as she never did, had never even been tempted to do. "As nice as this was, I really should go."

He grabbed her wrist and held her gently but firmly in place. "This might be a great many things, but nice isn't in the top fifty."

6

NODDING, Malina sat on the bed.

It was ridiculous to deny that sleeping with a colleague on a case was out of character. Carr was certainly too intelligent to buy that excuse.

"My life seems destined to be overly convoluted at the moment," she said. "And my work really is my life."

"You still have a right to be away from the job." He sat beside her. "I just want to be part of it. I want more than a one-night lay. Don't you?"

Hadn't she sworn to keep focused on her future? To toe the Bureau line and get her career back on track? And hadn't her mother shared her story of giving up her dreams of going to Paris to study art so she could stay in Kauai to run the family surf shop? Hadn't she vowed, to herself and her mother, that she would consider her decisions carefully and not compromise her goals?

But then nothing and no one had ever tempted her like Carr Hamilton.

"Yeah," she found herself saying. "I guess I do." She

smiled feebly. "I'd like to hang on to you for at least a week."

Thankfully, he returned her smile. "That long, huh?"

"I'm not much of a long-term woman."

An odd look crossed his face. He reached out and very gently tucked a strand of her hair behind her ear. "That's too bad. I'm a long-term man."

"But you'll settle for the rest of the night?"

He leaned toward her, his lips nearly touching hers. "For now."

She curled her hand around his neck, bringing him closer, giving over to the arousal he inspired.

Did she even have a choice in resisting him?

No matter how logically she tried to dismiss her need for him, the hunger refused to abate.

Frankly, she'd always thought the adage about not being able to help who you were attracted to was a bunch of romantic nonsense. You either chose to give in to your urges or not.

But as his mouth moved over hers, his tongue enticing and awakening every nerve ending in her body, she truly understood irresistibility for the first time.

Pressing her back into the mattress, he parted the shirt she wore—his shirt—cupping her breasts in his palms, his thumbs gliding over her distended nipples. She closed her eyes, absorbing the pleasure of him. A need she'd never felt with any other man washed over her, pulling her further under the spell of their desire.

She liked being surrounded by him. His clothes on her back; his body warm, bare chest brushing her front. As she wrapped her legs around him, the bulge of his erection met the heat between her thighs. He moaned against her lips, and she angled her hips, deepening the contact.

Even through the cloth of his pants, she could feel him pulse with raw lust, and yet, there was something inherently wonderful about holding back, taking time to let the hunger grow.

He drew his mouth down the side of her neck, leaving tingles in his wake. He moved slowly across her collarbone, sliding the tip of his tongue down, down until he reached her nipple. With barely a flick, he sent pleasure racing along her spine. She buried her fingers in his thick, silky hair, holding him against her as her heart rushed to keep up with the need building low in her belly.

Seeming to understand, he rocked his hips against hers. The friction sent a burst of pleasure through her. Still, she craved more.

She was a slave to his touch, and yet she knew he'd let her assert control in a heartbeat. There was comfort in that realization, deepening the bond she knew they already shared.

Briefly, he rolled away to ease out of his pants and take care of protection while she shrugged out of his shirt.

She sighed as his body rose over hers, as his lips glided across her cheek.

She welcomed him inside with a thrill of unfamiliar emotions and a flood of anticipation. He drew her arms over her head, his hands linking with hers as he moved in an easy rhythm, as if he could endlessly ride the waves of desire.

The tenderness in his touch was seductive, maybe even more so than the wild, aching climax from before.

As stimulating as talking to him could be, he didn't need words now. Breathy sighs and moans of longing and bliss were easy to read and respond to. As the pleasure rose and she chased fulfillment, she acknowledged she'd miscalculated. A week wouldn't be enough. Would a month? A year?

She gasped as she came, the powerful pulses draining her body and emptying her thoughts. Squeezing her hands, he followed, and she strained to hold on to the euphoria, the connection that seemed, at the moment, unbreakable.

When his breathing returned to a calmer rhythm, he rolled to his side and pulled her back against him. She shut out all questions and doubts, dragged the blanket on top of them and let sleep take her.

"OH, HELL, that's my cell phone."

Crawling to the end of the bed, Malina pawed through the heap of discarded clothes. She winced when she saw the number on the screen. "Malina Blair."

"Agent Blair, it's Sam Clairmont."

Double hell. It wasn't just the office calling, it was the boss. "Yes, sir."

"I'm interested in the progress of your case. Could you stop by the office later today and give me an update?"

"Yes, sir."

"In fact, it's curious you're not already here. You've worked every Saturday since you arrived."

The quiet, casual tone didn't fool her for a second. "Yes, sir. I know. I'll be there."

Heart pounding, she flipped the phone closed.

"Problem?"

Malina glanced back at Carr, who'd sat up, his

broad, bare chest exposed above the white sheet. "He knows."

"The SAC? About what?"

"About us." Naked, she leaped from the bed, then pulled on her dress from the night before. Damn. She'd have to go home and change first. "I gotta go."

"I'll take you."

After scooping her knife sheath off the floor, she glared at him. "I can handle this."

"I'm sure you can. I meant I'll take you to your car— it's still at my house."

"Right. Thanks."

He stepped into his pants, and she fought to ignore the fresh onslaught of lust. He did have the most amazing body. "And Sam can't possibly know about us. Don't let that silent stare of his get to you."

She forced herself back to the problem at hand—her supposedly all-important job. "He knows something's up."

"Admit nothing."

She glanced around, looking for the blond wig. "Thanks, Counselor." She didn't feel guilty about last night, she assured herself as she located the wig under the bed and stuffed it into her bag. What she did after working hours was nobody's business but her own.

Was she compromising her case by sleeping with Carr? Maybe. He was a witness. He could someday be called upon to testify in court.

And yet he was also part of the team, even if he wasn't an agent. The SAC knew she'd used Carr's connections—as well as the man himself—to work undercover at the party.

However, she didn't think he'd necessarily approve of the undercover work she'd done *after* the party.

Unfortunately, Carr was right—this thing between them was too powerful to deny. She wanted him enough to risk professional censure. There was no point pretending their relationship didn't matter a great deal.

She fastened her knife in its sheath to her thigh, then tugged her dress down to cover it.

Carr pulled the wig from her bag and handed it to her. "In case somebody's watching us."

"Right."

She should have thought of that herself. And she would have…eventually.

She needed coffee and a blisteringly hot shower before she faced the SAC.

After setting the wig, she headed through the cabin and outside. It was breezier and cooler than the day before, and Carr laid a jacket around her shoulders as he joined her on the dock.

She thanked him, and he smiled, looking a little distracted, as if he, too, was lost in thought about the turn their relationship had taken. He'd zipped up a black leather jacket over his own chest. No doubt the now buttonless shirt he'd worn yesterday would have been a bit exposing.

They didn't talk on the drive to his house, but Malina didn't find the silence uncomfortable. Carr might be able to discourse with the best of them, but he apparently knew the value of quiet as well.

As a woman who lived alone, had few female friends and worked in a male-dominated industry, she appreciated his restraint, or maybe, knowing Carr's successful record in court, his instinctive ability to read his audience.

"Would you come in a minute?" he asked as he helped her from the car.

"I still have to go home and shower and change."

"Please? I have something I'd like to give you in private."

She narrowed her eyes in suspicion, but nodded, then followed him inside. Truthfully, she was afraid of going back inside his spectacular house.

She might never want to leave.

As soon as she stepped across the threshold, she turned to him. "So?"

From his jacket pocket, he pulled out a plastic Baggie, which he handed to her. Inside the Baggie was a fingerprint card.

"They're Simon's," Carr said before she could ask. "He was very careful to hold on to the same glass all night. Did you notice?"

"I did." And she'd cursed the fact that she had no cause for a search warrant on Mr. Mystery and his floating cocktail party.

"I slipped into the master suite and lifted these off his hairbrush."

"You—" She ground her back teeth against the spurt of annoyance. "You could have been caught."

"But I merely wanted the full tour. I'm thinking of buying a similar boat myself."

She hated to admit he was so damn smooth, he'd probably pull off such a convenient excuse. She slapped the card against her palm. "This is also not admissible, Counselor." In fact, she was more than surprised he'd cast aside so many investigative rules—ones he had to be aware of.

"It doesn't have to be. I'm sure you're clever enough to get a warrant for prints and/or DNA if you need them later. Besides, I'm just an innocent and concerned civilian, offering my assistance to the overworked members of law enforcement."

"You think a judge and/or jury will buy that?"

"I can practically guarantee it." He grinned. "In the meantime, wouldn't it be interesting to see if Simon Ellerby is who he says he is."

"Have I mentioned this is my case?"

"Several times."

She glanced down at the card, then back at him. He'd done what she couldn't—or rather *wouldn't*—do. She was sticking hard and fast to the rules these days.

As unfamiliar as that idea was.

"Thank you," she said simply, tucking the prints in her bag.

"Good. I want payment."

FOR THE FIRST TIME since he'd met her, Carr knew he'd caught her completely by surprise.

Her eyes lit like blue flames. "No kidding. Payment?"

"Definitely." Before she could give in to the obvious urge to slug him, he grabbed her by her waist and pulled her against him.

He kissed her with an effort to remind her of what they'd shared and all that he wanted beyond the now.

Her body molded to his, her heat infused his veins.

Dear heaven, he wanted her, and the idea that she didn't want him as much was torture. He'd have to find a way to reach her, to convince her that a successful career didn't always lead to a happy life. That giving up everything for one thing was too great a sacrifice.

As he knew all too well.

Aware of her other obligations, he pulled back before

he wanted to, but he kept his hand against her cheek, knowing she'd retreat quickly.

She knocked his hand aside as she stepped back. "A kiss as payment?"

"Sure. I have money."

When she sighed, he closed the distance between them. "Take your evidence, talk to Sam, then come back here for dinner."

She looked skeptical. "You cook?"

"I'll make sure dinner is available," he clarified. "Come on. I'll be waiting all afternoon, wondering what you get from the print."

"Your larcenous print, you mean."

"Technically, larceny is taking something with the intent of depriving the victim of that item permanently. Simon still has possession of his fingerprints."

Saying nothing, she crossed her arms over her chest.

He was so crazy about that slightly annoyed, secretly amused look, he nodded. "Yes, that print."

Was he actually stooping to using the case as an excuse to see her?

Though, given the depths to which he'd stooped in the past, this one was positively virtuous.

"I'll be hungry later," she said finally.

"I'll be here."

In the open doorway, she turned back. "When I get brought up on charges of trespassing and tampering with evidence, I'm calling you to defend me."

"Naturally. It would be my great pleasure."

"SHE'S COMING?"

Nodding, Carr set his cell phone on the kitchen counter. "Finally," he said to his friend and neighbor, Andrea Hastings Landry.

Her husband, Tyler, sat at the chrome-and-glass table beside the house's rear windows. Beyond him, the landscape lights illuminated the pool and palm fronds blowing in the strong wind.

A storm was coming, and Carr would be glad to have Malina safely here with him. How he could be worried more about wind and rain and not diamond-stealing, gun-toting bad guys was a puzzle he ought to consider assembling.

Most likely, it was simply the fact that he was separated from her and the fear she wouldn't come back, which haunted him.

"You sure she's not a figment of your imagination?" Tyler asked, leaning back in his chair.

"Funny," Carr said, moving toward the windows to watch the dark clouds gather. "You should have gone into show business instead of law enforcement."

As Tyler opened his mouth to retort, Andrea interrupted. "Don't antagonize him, honey. I'm dying to meet this mystery woman who has our unshakeable Carr so twisted up."

Carr frowned. "I'm not twisted up."

Andrea patted his hand. "Oh, you so are." Her head angled, she regarded him thoroughly. "It's kind of cute actually."

"Oh, yeah, he's adorable," Tyler said as he grabbed his wife's hand and tugged her into his lap.

Tyler had once considered Carr a rival for Andrea's attention, even though she and Carr had never been more than friends. It seemed Tyler still hadn't let go of his jealousy completely.

As unsubstantiated as Tyler's feelings were, Carr

finally understood them. He wouldn't want another man near Malina either.

Hell, he *was* twisted up.

"She's not a figment of my imagination. She's…" How did he describe Malina in a way that was logical? He wasn't yet prepared to share the confusing and unfamiliar feelings he had for her. "Interesting," he said eventually. "Smart, resourceful, tough. You'll like her."

"Uh-huh," Tyler said, raising his eyebrows. "I didn't hear *hot* anywhere in that sentence."

"Of course she's—" Actually, *hot* seemed too tame. *Beautiful, exotic* and *compelling* were more to the point. "She's more than hot. That's too—" He broke off, shrugging.

"Oh, my," Andrea said, her eyes wide. "Carr, you never stumble over anything. What's going on?"

"Well, I'm not—"

"She obviously has a demanding job," Tyler broke in, directing his comment to Andrea. "And she doesn't live on the island."

"He's pretty much trolled the availability of all the women here," Andrea agreed.

"Maybe she's resistant to meeting Carr's friends. Maybe she's not that into him."

"She didn't show up for dinner. Maybe she has food issues." Andrea looked at Carr. "Does she?"

Carr made an effort to tuck his aggravation away and feign surprise. "Oh, you're going to include me in this psychoanalysis?"

Amused, Andrea nodded. "Sure. The patient is usually the best source of information."

"Usually," Tyler said, seeming skeptical.

And no doubt enjoying the digs at Carr's expense.

Carr leaned back against the windowsill. "Malina does have a demanding job, she doesn't live on the island. I have no idea whether she's resistant to meeting my friends, since I didn't tell her you were here. I also don't know if she has food issues—we've never shared a meal."

Speculation slid into Tyler's eyes. "And is she really into you?"

"I think so, but I don't think she's all that happy about it." Carr lifted his hands, then let them fall. "I'm not sure."

Andrea stared at him in shock. "You think so? You're not sure. You have no idea?" Her tone rose dramatically with each word.

"What the hell has this chick done to you, Carr?" was Tyler's pointed question.

Carr shook his head. "Realizing I'm repeating myself, I have no idea."

"So what does she do?" Andrea asked, compassionately passing over his out-of-character uncertainty.

"She's—" He stopped, realizing suddenly that his friends could help him figure out why he was so fascinated with Malina. A few days ago, he simply wanted to seduce her, and now he wanted a relationship. A serious one. Possibly.

Maybe Andrea and Tyler would understand the attraction in a way he couldn't. Hadn't they jumped quickly into their relationship? Hadn't it led to love and happily ever after?

He desperately wanted to know what it was about this woman that made her different from all the others he'd ever known.

Why was she so important? Why her? Why now?

She wasn't at all like a woman he envisioned himself

getting serious about. She was too direct. Though he was sure she understood and appreciated subtlety in other people, she didn't bother with it personally. Her toughness was sometimes harsh and unyielding. Necessary for her job, but could she turn it off and be tender? Would her sense of justice stand in the way of understanding his past, the way he used to live? And last, but certainly not least, she wanted off this relaxing island as fast as possible, and he wanted to be nowhere else.

He liked swords, and she was a .357 Magnum.

He refused to explain to Andrea and Tyler about who Malina was, what she did and what she represented in his life beyond what he'd already told them—she was a woman he'd recently started seeing whom he'd invited to dinner. He would explain to Tyler about the case if Malina wanted him to, but for now, he was keeping silent. Understanding the turn his life had taken in the past few days was essential, and he knew of nobody better to help him figure out the cause and consequences than his friends.

When the doorbell rang a few minutes later, he was grateful, as Andrea wasn't wildly patient when her curiosity was aroused.

She was, in fact, so inquisitive that she followed him down the hall to the front door.

Malina stood on the doorstep wearing the traditional government employee uniform—blue pantsuit, pressed white shirt, polished dark shoes. She'd pulled her hair back in a low ponytail, but she'd clearly been agitated at some point, since several strands had escaped to hang around her face, as if she'd run frustrated fingers through many times over.

"Sorry, I—" As her vivid turquoise gaze found

Andrea, her exhausted posture stiffened. "I'm clearly late. Too late."

She instinctively doubted him. Maybe she always would.

But as much as that possibility bothered him, he knew she had reason to doubt. She'd given the Bureau her blood, sweat and maybe even tears, and when she'd needed them most, they'd cast her aside to save face.

Before she could turn away, Carr wrapped his fingers around her wrist and tugged her inside. "I'm glad you're here. This is my friend and neighbor, Andrea Landry."

"Neighbor?" She directed her attention to Carr for a second, an apology clearly evident. "The sheriff's wife." She extended her hand to Andrea. "Malina Blair. Nice to meet you."

Andrea shook her hand, then her gaze flicked to Malina's side holster, exposed as her jacket fell open. "You're a cop?"

"FBI. Your husband's here?"

"He's in the kitchen."

"I'm going to need to talk to him," Malina said to Andrea, though she looked at Carr.

"I haven't said anything," he returned defensively.

She surprised him by sliding her hand down his arm. "Then it's time we did."

As Malina headed down the hall, Andrea gave Carr an elbow nudge. "FBI? You're dating an FBI agent? What's going on?"

Since he wasn't about to repeat the humiliating mantra of *I have no idea,* Carr shrugged and continued down the hall.

Tyler rose as they approached. In worn jeans and a red T-shirt, he didn't look much like the chief law enforcement official on the island at the moment, but then Carr was wearing nearly the same thing, except his T-shirt was white, so he probably didn't look much like a high-powered lawyer. Well, formerly high-powered.

The expression in both Tyler and Malina's eyes was all cop-to-cop as they exchanged introductions. Even without the sidearm, it seemed that Tyler would have certainly recognized her for what she was.

"We saved you some manicotti," Carr said as he joined them. "Are you hungry?"

Malina's gaze swept the room, full of chrome and glass, the black marble bar separating the kitchen from the dining area, then finally the backyard, ocean waves churning in the distance.

She assessed and evaluated with lightning speed, but Carr, used to reading people quickly, saw the pleasure and comfort that washed over her even before she smiled at him. "Starving. Thanks."

"Wine?" he heard Andrea offer as he headed to the fridge.

"Sure."

"Working on Saturday?" Tyler asked her.

Malina sat in the chair that faced the back of the house—and the ocean. "I've got a case that needs the extra time. Thanks," she added as Andrea set a glass of Chianti in front of her.

"You're not from South Carolina," Andrea said.

"No. Kauai."

"Yeah?" Andrea said. "I've always wanted to go."

"You've been to Prague and never to Hawaii?" Tyler asked, eyeing his wife with skepticism and pulling out the chair opposite Malina for Andrea.

"Anytime you want to take me, Sheriff, say the word." Andrea said sassily. "You look Hawaiian—sort of."

"My father's family goes back six generations. My mother's a California blue-eyed blonde, so I'm a mix."

"You work out of the Charleston office?" Tyler asked, returning to his seat on Malina's left. "You must know Rick Holly."

"Sure," Malina said. "He works Cyber Crimes. He's a good agent."

"What makes a good agent?" Andrea asked, her nosiness in full force as she leaned forward.

Carr set a plate of manicotti and salad in front of Malina. "Don't take offense. She's been trying to psychoanalyze me all night."

"Thanks," she said as she followed his movements. He sat next to her and saw her caution drop briefly. The connection between them sizzled, sparked to life by a glance. As much as he wanted Andrea and Tyler's opinion, he also wished—at that moment—that he was alone with Malina.

He probably shouldn't have unexpectedly thrown the friends in with their dinner date. His idea had been to get her to relax, not see him as the guy who simply wanted her in his bed, but as a whole person, one who wanted her in his life, not just his bed.

"We have an entire department at the Bureau dedicated to human behavior," she said as she turned back to Andrea. "They're way smarter than I am."

"So how did you get in?" Andrea asked, completely unabashed in her abrupt personal questions. "Federal law enforcement is extremely competitive."

Malina paused with her wineglass halfway to her lips. "Is it?"

"Sure."

Carr nearly intervened and explained about Andrea's

exposure to the police, beyond her husband, but he wanted to know the answer to the question. Sam hadn't given him Malina's recruitment history.

Malina's gaze never shifted from Andrea's. "See that landscape light in the top of that palm, third from the right on the left side of the pool?"

Andrea turned to view the light in question. "Yeah."

"I could draw my sidearm and shoot it out in less than fifteen seconds."

Everybody—with the exception of Malina, who continued to hold her wineglass casually in her left hand—jolted in surprise.

"Years ago," Malina continued, "one of the Bureau directors was on vacation in Kauai and happened to attend a bow-marksman tournament I participated in during high school. After I won, he gave me his card and said I should call him after I graduated from college. I did."

"So your greatest skill is shooting things?" Andrea asked slowly.

"No," Carr said automatically.

"Yes," Malina insisted.

Carr shook his head. "You're more to the Bureau than hired muscle."

"I have no problem being muscle," she said, shrugging. "That's where the action is. I spent the nearly five years of my career assigned to HRT."

"Hostage Rescue Team," Tyler supplied before his wife could ask. "The tactical division. Badasses."

Malina nodded—no arrogance or bragging, just acceptance of the truth. "Carr said you were a Marine. You worked with our guys at some point, I'm sure."

"Many times," Tyler said, his gaze intensifying in

his scrutiny of Malina. "They're a valuable asset in a crisis."

"Same to you." She toasted him with her wineglass. "Mostly we show up with storm trooper uniforms, a lot of firepower and attitude and scare the living crap out of the bad guys without a shot ever going off."

Carr found irrational fear blooming in his chest. Picturing Malina in black fatigues and a bulletproof vest wasn't exactly a comforting image. "And if the bad guys don't scare so easily?"

Malina forked up a bite of manicotti. "We're prepared for that, too. This is great, by the way," she added, glancing from Tyler to Carr to Andrea.

"Thanks," Andrea said. "I've been learning, since these guys would eat fried fish sandwiches and burgers at Coconut Joe's every night otherwise."

"Coconut Joe's?" Malina asked.

"The beach bar near the main pier." Tyler stroked his wife's cheek with his thumb. "We had our first date there."

Andrea's eyes widened. "We did *not*. That was a professional consultation."

"Really?" Carr put in. "He was certainly territorial. He didn't like that I was there."

While they launched into a discussion over just how shameless Tyler had been in his pursuit of Andrea the previous fall, Malina watched them curiously and finished her dinner.

Carr was distinctly aware of her and the information he'd learned about her past. A quiet island girl comfortable with extreme tension and the probability of violence. A woman raised in paradise who chose grit.

The contrast intrigued him.

Was it this contrast that drew him to her in a way

he'd never experienced before? Was it the unlikelihood of their contrasting paths ever merging that worried him?

He'd wanted to escape his quiet island life as well. He had enjoyed it with relish for a time, but he'd broken with his past and never wanted to go back.

Returning to the pulsing excitement of the city was her greatest ambition.

"Sorry, Malina," Tyler said, bringing her into the conversation. "It's an old argument."

"I wouldn't get too worked up over it, Sheriff," Malina said. "You obviously won."

Tyler nodded. "True. So...hot tub?"

"Smooth segue," Carr commented.

"We fed you women and sat through a polite chit-chat," Tyler said. "Don't we get a reward?"

Malina's lips twisted as she glanced at Carr. "Like a payment."

"I didn't say anything," he reminded her.

Andrea narrowed her eyes in her husband's direction. "What reward?"

"You two in bikinis in the hot tub," Tyler said, nodding for emphasis.

Malina leaned back in her chair. Carr was sure she would fire back at Tyler quickly. After all, he and the sheriff had done nothing but find glasses and open the wine for dinner. "I happen to have a bathing suit in the car, so I'm game for the hot tub on one condition."

"Name it," Tyler said as Carr recovered from the surprise of her response.

"I want to swim twenty laps in the pool first."

Tyler rose and held out his hand. "Deal."

As Malina reached out her hand, Andrea held up her finger. "I want to go to Hawaii."

Carr cleared away Malina's dishes and headed to the kitchen while Tyler sputtered in shock. "You have to admire her sense of timing."

Malina stood. "It's settled then. The hot tub is a perfect place to talk about stolen diamonds."

7

"DIAMONDS?" Andrea asked.

"Stolen?" Carr asked.

"Beer?" Tyler asked.

After Tyler filled beer and water orders from the poolside bar—complete with fireplace, wicker lounge chairs, full kitchen and giant grill—Malina let the warm water pound over her aching muscles while she gave the sheriff and Andrea the rundown on the case so far.

"You're right about Jack Rafton," Tyler said. "He doesn't have the balls for smuggling or theft."

"I'm not sure that Simon Ellerby does either," Malina said. "He's crafty enough, I guess, but major jewel thefts are generally instigated by organized crime groups, which are intricate, organized and brutal. Career thieves, on the other hand, are loners, resourceful and rarely violent. This gang—if there even is one— seems to fit with the latter profile."

"And yet you said stolen diamonds, plural," Carr pressed. "That seems to be a major theft."

Malina nodded. "It does. It turns out a remote diamond mine in Australia is missing a cache of stones.

No official report has been made to international authorities, but my boss made some calls to colleagues and learned that the theft is being kept quiet because a government official is suspected of being involved—in fact, they're all but positive it was an inside job. Law enforcement has the guy under surveillance and doesn't want anyone to know there's even been a theft, hoping he'll try it again." Malina could all but see giant rolls of red tape unspooling all over yet another small island. "So there's an internal investigation within the government and another one by the company that owns the mine."

Tyler sipped his beer. "Meanwhile, a whole lot of glittery stones are in the wind."

"And for more than a month," Malina said.

"They'll never recover them after all that time, will they?" To Malina's surprise, Carr directed this question to Andrea.

"I wouldn't think so," Andrea said. "I could check around about under-the-table diamond sales."

"You can, huh?" Malina asked, her surprise evident.

Andrea smiled with confidence. "I know some people, who know some people."

Malina's gaze sharpened. "No kidding."

"Andrea is an expert art appraiser," Carr said. "She works for a global insurance company and is often called in to determine the veracity of forgeries in theft cases."

Malina had easily determined that Andrea was intelligent and successful within five minutes of meeting her. She could also see the delicate-looking blonde wandering among dusty old art in museums, but it took a great deal of knowledge as well as technical skill and equipment to find fakes. "Are these thieves in jail? We don't want word leaking about the theft."

"They prefer the term *alternative architects*," Andrea said with a mischievous glint in her eyes. "And, no, they're not."

Malina glanced at Carr, who shrugged and drank from his water bottle. "Terrific. Thieves catching thieves." Surely her sarcasm was clear. "My job would be so much simpler if people either wore black or white."

"But it's the shades of gray that keep life interesting," Carr pointed out.

She pointed at him. "Don't think I don't realize you own a lot of gray suits." She let the jets massage her back for a few minutes in silence, then she inclined her head. "Sure. Why not. Ask," she said to Andrea. "I assume these guys are pros at being discreet."

"Definitely. I assume you can get me a list of the carats involved and the specifics of inclusions for each missing stone?"

"I'll copy it down for you," Malina said. "I'm pretty sure the SAC would object to me forwarding official, but secretly nonofficial, government reports."

"You could always transfer to the CIA," Tyler suggested.

Malina toasted him with her water bottle. "There's an uplifting thought."

"Any way to connect our local yacht captain Simon Ellerby to Australia?" Carr asked.

As he spoke, he slid his finger down her thigh. Even here, in the middle of crime solving—as unconventional as the setting was—he seemed to feel compelled to remind her of his physical presence.

As if she could forget.

Just as the rain overhead held off, the storm seeming to gather its strength before bursting, she sat beside him in a churning, intimate world of repressed need. With his flushed, handsome face close enough to touch, his husky voice sending shivers of anticipation rolling down her spine, she had to fight to concentrate, to hold off until she could find their intimacy again.

Unfortunately, she had a job to do. One that had never felt a burden until now.

She cleared her throat self-consciously, certain it had been a while since Carr had asked his question. "Simon Ellerby has several aliases—most of which are linked to minor jewel or art thefts."

"Oh, really," Carr asked, his tone full of innocence. "How did you learn that?"

Under the water, she grabbed his seeking hand, which had been wandering its way up her leg to her crotch. "I have my sources, too."

Tyler held up his hand. "I hate to throw cold water on such a warm night, but a theft in Australia linked to our little island here? What're the odds?"

"Really, really long," Andrea said.

Seeing as she was the expert, Malina accepted that assumption. But something about this case had her senses tingling—and not just because the object of her personal desire was within easy reach. "We can find no travel to Australia by Ellerby or any of his aliases."

"He could have sent an associate," Tyler said. "The guys you saw with Rafton."

"The thief could have sold them to somebody who sold them to Ellerby," Andrea added. "The farther down the line away from the origin the gems go, the less likelihood of tracing them to their source."

"But more people are brought into the fold," Carr said. "The chances of getting caught rise."

"What do your instincts tell you, Malina?"

Malina glanced across the bubbling water at Tyler as she considered his question. The immeasurable, undetermined, indistinctive evidence of a cop's gut. Only somebody who's looked into the eyes of a victim, then sat at their desk and stared at their computer late into the night, drinking bad coffee and praying for a break, could understand the trust and results that an instinct could bring.

It was drive, experience and desire rolled into one.

She trusted hers implicitly. "Australia and Palmer's Island shouldn't be connected, but I think they are."

"What do you want us to do?"

No hesitation, no question of support, no paperwork or official requests. There were big advantages to a small town that Malina had forgotten in the huge ocean of bureaucracy she'd chosen to wade through.

"Do you know a gem expert who could evaluate the one Carr and I found?" Going through Bureau channels could take weeks, and there was no way they had that kind of time. The diamonds would be sold soon, if they hadn't been already. To solve this case, she had to move fast.

Andrea nodded. "I know a guy in Charleston."

"I'll get you the evidence." Malina gave her a significant look. "To maintain the chain of evidence, you'll have to sign a statement, and I'll have to accompany you on the trip. Will that be a problem?"

"Nope." She high-fived her husband. "Back in the game."

Just as Malina was wondering if "the game" was a code word for illicit merchandise exchange and wondering how in the world Andrea and Tyler might be involved, Carr leaned over and whispered in her ear, "There's not a lot to do on this island."

"So, they—"

"They just want to help."

Malina shifted her gaze from Carr, to Tyler, then finally Andrea. "You people are strange as hell."

"It's part of our charm," Carr said.

Tyler toasted her with his plastic beer cup. "We also throw a great luau."

Thunder rolled in the distance, but everyone ignored it.

Malina was grateful. People—regular, ordinary people who wanted to protect their friends and neighbors—were a valuable commodity for a cop. A rare occurrence. It was almost comical in its honesty.

There were many who wanted to be "in the know" or to observe or speculate. But to participate in the process was rare.

"The cooperation isn't what you're used to, I guess?" Andrea asked.

"Not in D.C.," Malina acknowledged. And for the first time in a long time, she didn't feel the longing for the city she'd adopted and fought so hard to reach. The Bureau pinnacle. The escape from simple sunny days, mediocrity and obscurity.

Why couldn't she remember why that goal was so important?

She lifted herself out of the bubbling water. Sitting on the side of the tub, leaning back on her elbows, the stormy wind rolled over her, and she craned her neck back to stare at the tumultuous sky overhead.

Her gut, that infallible sense of right and wrong, was still talking, and she wasn't sure she was happy with the conversation. "But I understand island community all too well," she said, still watching the clouds sweep and gather overhead. "My childhood was full of it. I guess I just forgot how good it felt."

Warm, wet fingers linked with hers.

Carr.

She knew his touch as surely as she did her investigative instincts. That knowledge was both comforting and disturbing. She wasn't sure whether to clutch him like a lifeline or run as far and as fast as her feet would carry her.

"We're going to get through this," he said, his voice low and confident. "The case is as good as closed."

"My office may seem casual," Tyler said, "but we're serious about anybody who messes with us."

"As long as we're on the subject of true confessionals…" This time it was Andrea speaking. "How many calories does shooting burn?"

"Does that really have a place here?" her husband asked, clearly exasperated.

"Are you going to deny the power of those abs of hers?" Andrea returned. "Besides, I'm just trying to break the tension."

Clearly hearing them, Malina continued to watch the stormy sky. The blues, grays and shades of the blackest night swirled together. She wanted to make sense of it all. She wanted to prove herself more than anything, but not only to the Bureau brass. She wanted to close this case for the people of Palmer's Island. They wanted nothing more than a safe, happy, quiet life, and yet she knew they'd defend themselves and their neighbors at any sacrifice. They were the community every law enforcement agency wanted to be a reality, the one Malina, for one, had forgotten still existed.

Squeezing Carr's hand in silent thanks for giving her this moment, she pushed herself off her elbows and sat up straight. Her gaze moved to Andrea and Tyler. "Welcome to the team."

CARR HELD Malina's hand as they walked on the sand, their bare feet enveloped in rhythm by the rising and retreating Atlantic surf. With the cool air whipped up by the coming storm, he'd put on jeans and a white T-shirt, but she remained in her turquoise bikini, only adding a silky wrap around her waist.

Her indignation and determination no doubt kept her warm enough.

"Did you make the calls to Australia or did Sam?" he asked.

"He did. I'm too low on the bureaucratic pole to have powerful international connections."

"But he made the calls because you asked him to."

She slowed her stride. "Where is this going?"

"Just tell me. What led up to the calls?"

"I didn't think it was likely this was simply about smuggling diamonds. They're not illegal. The only reason to smuggle them is to avoid customs fees, like duties and tariffs, and they aren't large enough to warrant going outside the law. They're generally considered a cost of business and passed on in the price to brokers and end consumers. Diamonds are a valued commodity, transported with relative ease. Why take the chance of smuggling when you can simply add the cost into your selling price?"

"Unless you don't own the diamonds in the first place."

"Exactly."

"So you started researching diamond mines."

"It seemed the most logical place to start."

They walked on in silence a few minutes, then she glanced at him. "Your friends are really great."

The feeling was apparently mutual, since Andrea's parting whisper had been the same compliment for Malina. At least he knew for certain now that he wasn't crazy in noticing how special she was. "All part of the Palmer's Island package."

"You have something rare here."

He didn't think she was talking about herself, but the island. Still, he recognized both were true. "I know."

"I really appreciate your help with this case."

"You do?" At every opportunity, she'd told him he was interfering.

"I like to work solo, so I'm doing a lousy job of appreciating your insight. And I'd never understand this island so well without being part of it."

"It's important to understand the island?"

"Sure." She shrugged and he found himself distracted by the muscles that contracted at her shoulders. Andrea hadn't exaggerated—Malina's physique was lined with lean muscle.

Which he definitely wanted to get his hands on before the night was out.

"Basic victimology," she continued. "Know your victims, understand the guys targeting them."

Carr had employed the same tactics once in targeting juries. Life was indeed very ironic. "And what does our island tell you about the thief?"

"That he wanted somewhere quiet, completely unsuspecting. These gems are seriously hot, and he needed to get them as far away from their source as fast as possible. Also, this isn't a network of people who're used to working together."

"Jack Rafton."

"Exactly. He's drawn attention to himself. He's a wild card, one I'm sure Simon Ellerby aka Paul Galbano aka Stuart Costas, is kicking himself in the ass for bringing into the mix."

"Even though you gave us the information about violent, organized groups usually involved in jewel thefts, you think Simon is responsible?"

"I do."

"The cop's gut."

"That, plus the victimology I've already pointed out. Simon's a small-time thief who's branching out."

"And completely screwing it up."

"I don't know about that. We've got nothing on him yet, including his true identity."

"He has a lot of diversity in aliases."

"Smart. Most stick to one nationality. He works that silver hair, tan and vaguely European accent to his advantage." She stopped, staring at the storm clouds overhead. "And he just annoys the hell out of me."

"I can't imagine what that's like."

"Seriously." She turned to face him. "He likes doing all this under the sheriff's nose. He likes being mysterious. He absolutely loves having the president of the historical society on his yacht, asking him for donations, as if he's a member of legitimate society. *I bought Le Bijou here sight unseen on the recommendation of a colleague,*" she mocked, cocking her head from side to side. "*A mere whim.* What a lot of blowhard crap. He makes me want to shoot something."

He winced. "Sorry to be a downer, but I'd rather this didn't come down to who has the most firepower."

"Yeah." She sighed, visibly bringing her anger

under control. "I'll do my best, but I'm not promising anything."

"Speaking of firepower...HRT?"

For the first time, he saw a hint of uncertainty in her eyes. "Yeah. Not too sexy, I guess."

"It is. And yet scary at the same time. You're not..." He slid his hands down her arms, then gripped her hands. "Is that why you want to go back to D.C.? To be part of HRT?"

"No way. I want to run the place." She grinned suddenly. "It's about time a woman was in charge."

"Of the entire Bureau?" His tone climbed in surprise.

"Sure. Why not?"

'Cause that's too damn far away. "I—" He cleared his throat in the face of that fierce stare. "No reason. I just...if you were HRT, you must be good at working on a team. Don't you like that?"

"I was in command most of the time."

His heart sank. "Oh."

She scowled. "Still, the leadership has to deal with politics as much as procedure. I'm lousy at that part."

"True. I can't imagine you networking at cocktail parties and making under-the-table promises to special-interest groups." How shameless had he become? Discounting her abilities so she wouldn't leave him? It was pathetic. "Your strength of character is one of the things I admire most about you," he added at the urging of the little conscience he had left.

"Uh-huh." She slid her hands up his chest, wrapping her arms around his neck. "You're not just saying that to get me in bed, are you?"

"Certainly not."

"No way, Counselor. That righteous indignation may impress juries, but I know you too well."

With her pressing her nearly naked body against him, Carr found it hard to concentrate, much less lie. A feat he previously considered impossible. And though he'd done some despicable things in the past, he considered trying to lure her and hold her to his side—when he didn't remotely deserve a hero like her—one of his worst.

Considering how instinctively she kept pulling away, she must suspect his stellar record in court had come via both fair means and foul. But if she knew everything… if she realized his worst…she'd sprint in the opposite direction.

He wrapped his arms around her. "Is it so devious to want you with me? To want to spend time with you?"

"No, and I'm done questioning how right we are to-gether, even though we seem to be on different paths." When he frowned, she added, "You want to understand why I want to go back to D.C. so badly, and I want to know why you left Manhattan."

He stiffened.

"Or maybe not so different." She pressed her lips against his, gently seeking. "Enjoy now. Today. This moment. You never know when you'll have another chance."

How well he knew that truth. Hadn't the realization of limited time changed his life?

Repent of selfishness, Sister Mary Katherine was always saying. Wasn't that his desperate goal? Didn't he want Malina to have everything she wanted, even if the result came at his expense?

Yes. But he wasn't about to give up easily on the

dream that he could have it all. Even if he deserved nothing.

Regardless, he had no chance resisting her touch.

Her mouth moved over his; her tongue slid past his lips to entice him beyond reason. He cupped the back of her head with one hand, the other gripping her backside, molding every part of her to his neediness.

His erection pulsed against his jeans. He could hardly believe this beauty, this extraordinary woman, wanted him and allowed him to touch her. And yet, his body overrode any sense his mind might have made of reality.

Addiction came in all forms, and she was his.

Her hands moved to the hem of his T-shirt, which she drew over his head. With him naked to the waist, she pressed her cheek briefly to his bare chest. The simple intimacy had him coming unglued on many levels, not the least of which was sexual.

Then she kicked her heel against his calf.

They both fell to the sand below with an abrupt thud, and by the time he'd recovered his breath she was already stripping off her bikini top. She leaned down, kissing him again, and her bare breasts teased his chest, sending a shot of acute hunger through his body like a rocket launch.

With a lift of her hips, she'd shimmed out of her suit bottom and wrap, then, straddling him, she unfastened the buttons on his jeans. Her hand found his erection, and within a stroke he'd flopped back on the sand, completely helpless to her needs, like a fish waiting for the surf to take him under.

Thunder rumbled overhead. She moved her hands over his body, up and down, over and across. Kissing him with the same wild urgency, the very elements heard her call as raindrops plopped hard and insistent against their skin.

A storm on the coast gathers and builds as no other place on earth. It draws from land and sea until the water seems to boil with its intensity and the sand on the shore contracts, bracing itself for the onslaught.

She arched her back and glanced at the sky. The rain fell harder, and when her gaze found his again, she was laughing.

"Back pocket," he managed to gasp.

She found the condom and applied it with haste, then she lifted her hips over his erection and plunged down before he could fully acknowledge the wet onslaught from the heavens.

With an intense rhythm, she pumped her hips against his. His heart raced, seeming to want to jump out of his chest. Her breathing hitched.

Gasping, she climaxed, her inner walls gripping him, urging him to follow. As he instinctively closed his eyes to absorb the spike of pleasure, he buried his hand in the glossy wetness of her hair and brought her face to his. His kiss was grateful and desperate at the same time as he followed her into the glory of completion.

8

THEY RAN through the storm into the house, water dripping everywhere, sand grating in a variety of crevices.

Carr insisted on a shower to warm up and clean up, and Malina could hardly resist. With water dripping off his lashes, his brown eyes full of satisfaction and laughter, she was certainly willing to go with the suggestion.

"You know the only bad thing about you in a bikini?"

"No."

"I kind of like disarming you."

He shampooed her hair, then pressed her against the tiled wall, her legs wrapped around his hips.

His erection pressed between them, rocking against her, never entering, teasing her to near madness. He kissed her neck, brought her nipples to painful buds with his thumbs then completed his pleasurable torture by yanking a towel off the rack outside the shower and drying her from head to toe.

Drugged with need, she let her head drop back

over his arm as he lifted her and carried her to the bedroom.

She was a slave to the wild desire he inspired. Did he even have to touch her to make her come? Probably not, but his touch was pretty damn amazing, so she wasn't about to question success.

Lying on his bed, she watched almost in slow motion as he loomed over her. Something primal and possessive flashed in his eyes. When he entered her, it was apparent he'd already taken care of protection.

When he'd done that, she had no idea. He had a way of overwhelming, exciting and caring all at the same time. And never had she been so happy to lose control.

He'd left the windows open, and rain lashed at the glass, spraying through the screens. Lightning flashed in unexpected bursts as the wind howled, tossing the white gossamer drapes back and away from the walls. She was at the center of a maelstrom, one only they could feel but that nature had provided a backdrop for.

Wrapping herself around him mind and body, she met each thrust with the realization that the acceptance she craved was fulfilled in these intimate moments with him. She wanted the building and heightening to go on and on, almost fearing this time would bring even more pleasure than the last, and she'd become dependent. But his skill and their chemistry were too powerful to deny for long. All too soon, the spiral of need deep inside tightened, then burst, casting rhythmic pulses over them both until he collapsed on top of her, his breath coming in satisfied gasps.

"If the storm takes us, at least I'll die a happy man," he said after a time, flopping on his back next to her.

She found the energy to pat his bare chest. "Same goes."

He made her feel fluid and womanly and vulnerable in a way she never had before. She'd never let anyone so close, and the idea of him being the one who could affect her so strongly worried her. They were going in opposite directions; their goals—other than closing this case—weren't remotely similar.

They could never last.

To distract herself from her troubling thoughts, she glanced around the bedroom. It was somehow warm and modern at the same time. The wood floors were stained a dark cherry, and an antique settee rested in one corner. The walls were pale gray, the bed frame a streamlined polished steel and the comforter light blue.

Through the skylight overhead and the windows along the back wall, the unrelenting rain continued to pound.

An elaborate sword in a glass case, hanging on the wall by the door, attracted her attention. She turned on her side and propped her head in her hand. "Where'd you get the sword?"

"An auction in New York."

"Any particular reason it attracted your attention?"

"I like swords," he said, his gaze riveted to the object in question.

"You were a fencer, right?"

"I was."

It was rare for Carr to be uncommunicative. She wasn't sure whether he wanted her to be quiet or to leave, or whether he was simply tired.

He seemed to come out of his silent trance and pushed off the bed. "You're probably getting cold." He pulled back the bed covers, then swept her up in his arms, sliding her beneath the sheets with all the ease of a father and child's bedtime ritual.

It was oddly comforting and arousing at the same time.

Joining her, he tucked her against him and kissed the top of her head. "You prefer guns, I guess."

"Damn straight."

"They're cold and not very pretty."

"They're functional. Appearance doesn't apply."

"You have a Glock nineteen, polymer finish. No stainless steel?"

She snorted. "Flashy. Nobody with any decent skill carries one of those things."

"But appearance doesn't apply."

Caught in her own judgment, she asked, "This relates to swords how?"

He turned his head to meet her gaze. "Have you noticed we're very different?"

"Have you noticed we have some very unusual conversations?"

"I thought I was the only one who'd realized it." He returned his attention to the sword. "It's called a *jian,* a double-edge sword known in Chinese folklore as the gentleman of weapons. The earliest records have them mentioned as far back as the seventh century BC. This one was made nearly two hundred and fifty years ago. I thought it was historic and lovely, almost mesmerizing."

"But still deadly."

"Certainly." But he frowned, as if he hadn't considered the brutality of the weapon. "I think of it as elegant."

"I do, too. I mean, I don't think I'd hang a gun on

the wall of my house as a decoration. It's a tool I need to do my job effectively, not a piece of art."

"You don't have a gun collection?"

"No. Do you have a sword collection?"

"Just the one."

"Ditto." She paused, reconsidering. "Well, I do have a clutch piece I used to wear back in my HRT days, but I haven't carried it in years."

"Why not?"

"Haven't needed it," she said slowly, realizing she'd been so busy chasing high-profile offenders and trying to make a name for herself in the Bureau, she'd stayed off the streets and out of the action in other ways.

She liked investigating, solving the puzzles. She liked the heightened awareness she always experienced in those last moments of tracking down and arresting the subject who'd caused so much turmoil. She was proud of the way her mind and body went eerily calm in the middle of a crisis.

That sense of adventure was what had drawn her into law enforcement in the first place.

Her marksmanship had simply been the ticket.

But she couldn't deny she missed HRT. The sheer physicality of the constant training was always a challenge. Keeping mind and body in top shape was essential, and she was skilled at both.

"Still think this is an unusual conversation?" Carr asked.

"Ye— Maybe not. At least not for us. You're telling me we're not so different. We just use different methods to get to the same place."

"Ah…actually, I was trying to point out I'm subtle and you're obvious."

"You're…" She sat bolt upright. "I'm what?"

"Not that obvious is a bad thing," he hastened to explain. "You look pretty damn cute in your blue suit and sidearm."

"Cute?" She was sure her blood, literally, was on the verge of boiling. "I've never been cute at any time in my life."

"Even when you had braces in middle school?"

"I didn't have braces."

"Really? Well, nice teeth, then." He cleared his throat. "I actually like your assessment of our situation much better than mine. We're different simply because we go about things in a different way."

"Exactly." She narrowed her eyes. "You talk things to death, and I—"

"You stare people down until they crack under the pressure."

"Now you're just trying to suck up."

"Is it working?"

"Not really."

"Then you must be missing something in the delivery." He wrapped his arm around her waist and tugged her down to lie alongside him. "You challenge me in ways I've never experienced with anyone else. I rarely find myself caught off guard and yet you always surprise me."

"You do read people well."

"But you're a tough one." He kissed the corner of her mouth, and she breathed in the now familiar sandalwood scent of his skin—so seductive, easily soothing the ragged edges of her temper. "I want to know you, to understand you."

"As much as you want me naked in your bed?"

"As much as."

Definitely scary. She'd stepped into completely unfamiliar territory, an area where her training held no power.

She stared into his eyes, dark, probing, unfathomable. And leaped into the abyss. "Then it should be obvious what I need right now."

CARR WOKE to ringing.

As Malina groped for her cell phone on the bedside table, he commented, "Is this going to be a thing?"

She jabbed him briefly with her elbow before answering, so when he realized the caller was business— obvious by the sudden formal clarity of her voice—he took great delight in placing lingering kisses against her neck and shoulders while she talked.

He was entirely annoyed, however, when he heard the words "I'll be right there," which caused him to clutch her back tighter against his chest.

Their stormy, sensual night couldn't be ending. The reality of the case they'd yet to solve, the possibility that she'd—again—find a reason to pull away from him wasn't something he wanted to face.

He was in serious trouble with this woman.

"Do you have any idea who that was?" she asked as she sat up and snapped the phone closed.

Not only didn't he know, he didn't much care. It seemed selfishness wasn't an impulse that could be easily cast aside. "Do you? I was hoping my distraction was actually distracting you."

"The freakin' mayor."

"Harvey?"

She nudged his shoulder before leaping from the bed. "Not yours, Counselor. Mine." Naked, she strode into the bathroom. "Well, mine for now."

Carr buried his face in his pillow. After his blundered

attempt last night to get her to talk about their differences, which was supposed to lead to a discussion of their future and feelings, he hardly needed a reminder that she was only his temporary lover.

When he heard the shower running, he knew his fantasy of making love, followed by omelets and a bare-skin swim in his heated pool was just that.

Rolling out of the bed, he snagged his pants off the floor and put them on before walking into the bathroom.

She was already in the shower.

He literally clenched his fists at his sides to keep from reaching for the shower door and joining her. "It's Sunday morning. Doesn't he have babies to kiss, lies to tell and preachers to impress?"

"Probably. But his dog is lost. Again, I might add."

Carr, his mind supplying vivid images of Malina's amazing body under the stream of hot water barely two feet away, braced his forehead against the wall and fought for control. "His dog?"

"Pooky. The family Maltese. He's been kidnapped before, so the kids are a mess." She paused, then the water shut off and the towel hanging over the shower door disappeared. "Seriously, they couldn't possibly have hired another dog walker with a record, could they?"

"I, for one, have no idea. But I'm about to make it my mission in life to be sure they never do again."

The shower door popped open, and Malina's head poked out. A fog of hot air billowed around her. She'd piled her hair on top of her head, but her face and body were dewy with steam.

He closed his eyes. The things he did for his soul's respectability.

She grabbed him and kissed him at the base of his throat, then wrapped the towel around her body. "You should come. You charm everybody within miles, and a puffy white dog shouldn't be a stretch to find."

"Can I ask a very obvious question?"

"Ha," she said as she stood at the bathroom sink and pawed through her bag. "I thought you were the subtle one."

"How can I charm a dog that's missing?"

Pausing in the process of applying mascara, she looked at his reflection in the mirror. "No, you're charming the kids—twins, a boy and a girl. You know, good cop, bad cop."

"You're the bad cop, I take it."

"Definitely," she said, snagging her suit off the hanger she'd hooked to the towel rack the night before.

All in all, he preferred the blue bikini, but she was inviting him along on this odd quest and, by definition, inviting him into her life, so he'd be crazy to argue.

"Why are we doing the good cop, bad cop routine with a couple of kids?" he asked as they climbed in her car a few minutes later.

"Because they kidnapped the dog."

"You think so?"

"Pretty sure. Their parents are fighting. There was a rumor of their dad cheating, which I personally think is crap, but they decided to take drastic action. A lot of attention focused on them, the family gathered around, sticking together to find sweet little Pooky—it's a pretty smart way to have some family-bonding time, if you think about it.

"Anyway, I gave them my card and cell phone number when I found the dog the first time, so—"

"Hang on." Carr held up his hand. "The first time

you found him? *You* solved the case of the mayor's kid-napped dog?"

"Yeah. The dog walker did it. Though that butler did have some beady eyes, so I kept a close watch on him, too."

Carr remembered reading about the feel-good story in the newspaper. The FBI had been called in, and the case had been solved within hours. Now he knew why the agent in charge had refused to be interviewed for the story. "Sort of a step down from interrogating a SEC-violating senator's son, wouldn't you say?"

She winced. "Thanks for reminding me."

"So you want to explain why you're so happy to save little Pooky again?"

"Hey, I might have suffered great humiliation in front of my shortsighted colleagues, but having the mayor on my side can only be a good thing. Besides, it'll be fun." Looking gleeful, she exited the Ravenel bridge and headed into downtown Charleston. "Interrogating a couple of ten-year-olds, causing a scene in the neighbor-hood. I can't think of any better way to spend a Sunday morning."

"I can."

"Men," she sighed, "always thinking with their pe-nises."

"I didn't hear many complaints from you last night."

Smiling, she glanced over at him. "Good point."

Carr might have wanted sex, but he knew when to play the cards he'd been dealt. While the mayor and his family were bonding, Carr would be doing some bonding of his own. The fact that Malina trusted him enough to bring him into her work without him having to beg, cajole or insist was definitely a positive sign for their relationship.

When they turned off King Street into the gated driveway of the mayor's historical three-story mansion, complete with impressive Venetian-style palazzi at each level, it was apparent that he hadn't called the cops or the press this time. After all, one dog-napping was a feel-good story, but a second was an embarrassment.

The security detail met them at the gate, checked their IDs, then allowed Malina to park before they were escorted to a side door.

Just inside, Mayor Don Parnell paced the hall in a rumpled charcoal suit. "Thank goodness you're here, Agent Blair." The mayor shook Malina's hand, then his tired gaze moved to Carr. "And Mr. Hamilton, good to see you again."

"Carr happened to be with me when your call came in, sir," Malina explained as the security guards closed the door behind them.

The mayor nodded. "Excellent. He helped out First Presbyterian last year when some jerk staged a fall down the front steps, then tried to sue the church for ten million dollars. Mr. Hamilton cleared the whole thing up nicely."

At Malina's impressed glance, Carr nodded modestly. His charity knew no bounds—and it shouldn't, according to Sister Mary Katherine. Still, he didn't think it was wrong to take some credit in front of the woman he was trying to romance.

"It's hard to believe we're back in this position so soon," Parnell continued. "My wife is a wreck."

"And the kids?" Malina asked.

"They can barely stop crying, and they won't let my wife and me out of their sight. They're afraid one of us is going to be next."

Malina exchanged a knowing look with Carr.

Clearly frustrated, the mayor speared his hand through his wavy brown hair. "The only way they'd let me leave the room is because I told them it was you. How could this happen *again?* We don't even have a dog walker anymore."

"Well, I'd like to talk privately with you before we go back to your family." Malina slid her hands calmly into her pockets and faced the mayor. Her voice was confident and quiet. "When did you notice Pooky was missing?"

The mayor stopped pacing and mirrored her pose. "This morning," he said, his tone more controlled than before. "I got up about six-thirty. Pooky always hears me and comes out of one of the twins' rooms, meeting me at the top of the stairs. This morning, no Pooky. I looked everywhere, had the security detail hunting through the bushes, driving down the street.

"When it was apparent she was gone, I had no choice but to wake up my wife and the twins. Madison and Edward insisted I call you. What else could I do? They were hysterical."

"I'll bet," Malina said. "When was the last time you saw Pooky?"

"Sometime after dinner last night." He waved his hand vaguely in the direction behind him. "The kids took her out to play in the backyard."

"Did you see them come back in?"

"No, but I heard them."

"You heard the dog bark?"

Parnell looked thoughtful. "No, she's not much of a barker. I heard the kids come back in."

"Has it occurred to anybody that Pooky might have simply gotten out and run off?" Malina asked.

Parnell shook his head. "She can't. We have an

electric fence, remember? As long as she's wearing her collar, she can't cross the property's barrier without getting shocked. You've seen her, high-strung, tiny little ball of fur. She won't go anywhere near the edge of the yard."

"Oh, right," Malina said. "I'd forgotten."

But it was apparent to Carr that she hadn't overlooked that detail at all. She was leading the mayor somewhere, and Carr, for one, couldn't wait to find out how she'd get there without insulting him and jeopardizing her powerful connection.

Crossing her arms over her chest, Malina stepped closer to Parnell. "Besides the fence, Mr. Parnell, you also have a security detail with you twenty-four hours a day. How do you suppose the dog-napper got access to the property, not to mention your kids' bedrooms?"

Parnell stiffened. "Agent Blair, I'm not sure I like your tone. What are you suggesting?"

"An inside job."

"Not me certainly."

"No, the twins."

Her flat delivery was a wake-up call to Parnell. His head snapped back, and he rubbed his temples as if he could reach inside his head and physically clear his thoughts.

"I don't hear you arguing against that theory," Malina said after a few seconds of silence during which the mayor returned to his pacing.

"They're not really criers," Parnell said with a sigh. "Especially not Edward. But every time he looked at his sister and saw her crying, he started up, too. It seemed strange."

Malina angled her head. "Kids do strange things to attract attention sometimes."

The mayor's face flushed with embarrassment. "I'll bet most of them don't involve calling the FBI, though."

"I don't see any reason to make an official report, but I think they ought to try excelling at baseball or soccer or singing in the choir rather than learning to cry and manipulate on command."

Parnell smiled weakly. "How about the drama club?"

"There you go." Malina's gaze locked on Parnell's. "How do you feel about letting the consequences of their actions play out?"

The mayor looked from Malina to Carr. "How?"

After a minute or two of whispered planning, the mayor led them down the hall to the den, where the kids and their mother were waiting.

"Excellent work," Carr whispered in Malina's ear as they walked. "The everything's-under-control tone and the composed body language were nice touches."

She shrugged away the compliment. "Don't even think about stealing my technique for your next appearance in court."

"I'll do my best."

"One last thing…" Malina said as they approached the doorway. "Where's the butler?"

Parnell angled his head. "Stevens? Sunday's his day off."

Malina patted his shoulder. "Just checking."

When they entered the posh den, Madison and Edward Parnell, both blue-eyed blonds and still wearing pajamas, sat on either side of their mother on the sofa. Their faces were red and puffy from crying, but Carr was certain he saw little Madison's eyes gleam as she noticed Malina.

"I'm sorry we have to see each other again under these difficult circumstances," Malina said formally to Mrs. Parnell, who rose to shake both Malina's and Carr's hands.

"I really don't understand how this could happen again," she said somewhat desperately, her gaze seeking out her husband's.

Uncertainty and fear permeated the room, and the mayor, either from embarrassment or lack of compassion, didn't seem to sense his wife's anxiety. He stood apart from the family.

"I have a pretty good idea," Malina said to Mrs. Parnell. "I've examined the crime scene thoroughly, but I'm going to need to talk to the kids now."

"But, I—"

"It's okay, Lorene," Parnell said, interrupting his wife. Somewhat hesitantly, he extended his hand to her. She grabbed it like a lifeline, and they retreated to the other side of the room.

From their gestures and expressions, Carr assumed the mayor was explaining the plan.

Facing the kids, now alone and uncertain, Malina wasted no time in putting on her bad cop gear. "I brought an attorney with me," she said, jabbing her thumb over her shoulder to indicate Carr. "You should have one present when you're questioned by the police."

In sync, two pairs of bright blue eyes widened. "Q-questioned?" Madison ventured to ask.

"Sure," Malina said, placing her hands on her hips. "You wanted the cops, you got 'em."

Carr acknowledged that Malina looked wildly intimidating in her dark suit. Plus, when she moved her hands to her hips, she revealed her holstered pistol.

This isn't a woman to mess with was clearly the message.

Understanding his role, Carr stepped aggressively between the kids and Malina. "There's no need to intimidate my clients, Agent Blair. They're cooperating, aren't they?"

As he looked back toward the kids for confirmation, they nodded slowly.

Sitting next to Edward, knowing he was the weak link in this conspiracy, Carr glared at Malina. "Please continue, Agent—as long as you can keep your questions soothing and nonthreatening."

Malina looked disdainful. "I'd certainly hate to be threatening when there's a criminal to be unmasked, Counselor."

Carr forced himself to appear appalled. "An innocent dog's life is at stake, Agent Blair. Surely you don't intend to—"

"Where were you two last night at seven-thirty?" Malina demanded, her glare jumping to Madison.

"W-we took Pooky in the backyard to play," the little girl said, reaching out to clutch Carr's hand like a lifeline.

How Malina continued to glare into that innocently beautiful—and now terrified—face, Carr had no idea, but he supposed they didn't let wimps into HRT.

"Did you see anyone in the backyard?" she asked.

"Well, we—" Madison glanced over at her brother. "No, no we didn't."

Malina, not missing a beat, loomed over the girl. "That, Madison, is a big, fat…lie."

As Madison burst into tears, which may have actually been genuine this time, Edward leaped to his feet.

"Pooky's fine! Nobody kidnapped her. We gave her to my friend Alan to take care of and pretended she was missing and it was all Madison's idea and she made me do it so it's not my fault!"

9

MALINA WALKED with Carr and the mayor to her car.

"Thanks for all your help," the mayor said. "I certainly hope this is the first—and last—stunt the twins pull."

"Anytime, Mr. Mayor." With the door open, Malina braced her foot against the frame. "And I hope you and your wife work things out. You make a nice couple."

Parnell nodded and turned away, but before Malina could drop into the driver's seat, he'd faced her again. Uncomfortable and hesitant, he asked, "How'd you know we were having problems?"

"You asked your security detail to help you look for Pooky, which tells me you're not in the habit of turning to your wife in a crisis. You don't want to bother her or worry her, or maybe you simply don't want to include her." Malina shrugged. "Plus this stunt the twins pulled was a big neon sign."

Parnell ducked his head. "I stay pretty busy."

"Of course. You have a high-pressure—"

"I didn't have an affair," Parnell interrupted defiantly.

Malina held up her hands. "None of my business." She lowered her voice, partly because she was in no position to give advice and partly hoping surveillance on the grounds wouldn't pick up her words. "But you have a nice family. I'd find a way to hang on to them."

As she settled into her sedan, Malina glanced at Carr. Her family was nearly five thousand miles away, and she could think of nobody she'd rather spend time with than the man next to her. "It's not every day you open and close a case within two hours. I say we celebrate. How about lunch?"

He leaned across the console and kissed her softly. "Sounds perfect."

At the all-you-can-eat crab-and-oyster bar they found in downtown Charleston, they talked about their childhoods, the singularly unusual bond of growing up on small-town islands. They had the same experience of littering tourists, rowdy tourists and tourists in search of historical and naturalistic experiences—as well as the unmistakable knowledge that those tourists kept their economy in the black, whatever the drawbacks.

Once, Malina tried to broach the subject of why Carr had left Manhattan, but he brushed over his move from high-powered litigator to partially retired defender of churches and charities as if it was simply the natural evolution of a lawyer's career.

She'd faced too many cold-eyed sharks in court to know that wasn't remotely true, but she didn't see how she could probe him for answers when she was determined to hold back herself.

As they rose to leave the restaurant, Malina linked their hands. "So, Counselor, got any ideas on how we could spend the rest of the afternoon?"

Grinning, he held open the door. "A few."

Outside stood a woman, about sixty, with silver hair and wearing an expensive-looking plum suit. She thanked Carr for holding the door open, then paused, staring at him. "Carr Hamilton?" she asked, her face going white with shock.

"Yes, ma'am, are you—"

She slapped Carr across his face. "You killed my husband!"

Malina's instincts kicked in the next instant. She jumped between them. "I'm sure there's been a mistake."

The woman moved forward as if she wanted to hit Carr again, and Malina snagged her arm, pressing her gently but firmly against the wall outside the restaurant. "Don't even think about touching him again."

"Malina, please." Carr grabbed her waist from behind and pulled her away from the woman. "She—" His voice broke. "Just let her go."

Stunned, Malina turned to watch her lover head down the block toward the parking lot where they'd left her car.

"He killed my husband," the woman in front of her insisted.

Malina stepped back and eyed her with distinct suspicion. Carr had been a profitable litigator in New York. He'd successfully argued many cases against big corporations throughout the country. There were bound to be people who didn't like the outcome of the judgments.

"I'm not sure what happened to you," Malina said finally, backing away, "but Carr wasn't the cause."

The woman lifted her chin. "But he was. *Aberforth versus Bailey Industries,* here in Charleston, five years ago. Look it up."

Then, with regal bearing, she headed into the restaurant.

Malina fought to calm her racing heart.

She braced her hand against the restaurant's brick wall. Carr's hurt and guilty eyes flashed in front of her.

There were plenty of horrors in her past. All of them job-related. Justice was sometimes bloody, often unpleasant, but Carr would never knowingly hurt anyone.

No way.

But then why had he gone from the glory of being on the short list as the attorney most feared by global insurance companies and high-powered consumer products corporations to defending churches against fraud?

Honesty and truth are two entirely different concepts, he'd said. And once she'd asked him, *Do you ever feel guilty for making that money on the tide of pain and suffering your clients have to weather?*

As her stomach clenched, she spun around and headed toward the car. There had to be an explanation. A man who'd gone to so much trouble to stand against smugglers and thieves wouldn't—

He stood for justice and integrity.

A sense of righteous assurance filled her, driving her to the parking lot.

Carr stood by the passenger door. His expression was closed, remote, unapproachable.

Malina swallowed the lump trying to form in her throat. "You can't please everybody, I guess."

All the way back to his house, she kept a running, inane and one-sided commentary going on cases she'd worked where the victim whose ass they'd just saved wanted to sue the Bureau. People were odd, blah, blah.

You just can't predict what somebody who's been through a traumatic experience will do afterward, et cetera.

Carr said nothing. He stared out the passenger side window.

She knew she was bungling the situation badly but had no idea how to adjust. It gave her a whole new respect for people who had to deal with her when she was moody and distant. No wonder they annoyed her further by babbling like idiots most of the time.

When she shifted the sedan into Park in Carr's driveway, he got out and came around to her side to open her door. He held out his hand to assist her but immediately let her go when she'd gained her feet.

Fear and uncertainty consumed her as she followed him inside.

He strode straight to the living room and poured a crystal tumbler of whiskey, no ice.

"It's only three o'clock," she said, her nerves clanging with alarm. "A little early for that, don't you think?"

He shrugged, sipped and headed over to the windows at the back of the room.

She approached him, having no idea what she was going to say but knowing she had to do something. "Look, Carr—"

"Have you ever killed anyone?" he asked, his back to her as he stared out the windows.

The knots in her stomach twisted tighter. "I have."

"Shot, I guess."

"Yes."

He downed the whiskey in one gulp. "I've killed, but with nothing so clean as a bullet to the heart."

Malina laid her hand on his shoulder, rubbing the knotted muscles, wishing she could find the right thing to say to comfort him. "Whatever happened, I'm sure you did what you could."

He shook his head. "Do you remember their faces, the ones you've killed?"

"No," she said, mirroring his quiet tone. "The lost innocent haunt me, not the dead and the guilty."

"What about the guilty who continue to live?"

Had one of his clients died over the stress of a trial? Had one of the defendants? "Whose—"

"Me!" he shouted, spinning around, his beautiful face harsh with anger and pain. "*I'm* guilty."

"Of what?" Malina demanded. "Everybody's done things they're not proud of, Carr. You learn from your mistakes and move on. Trying to change the past is futile. Look at me, nearly ruining my career because of blind ambition. So I get dumped in Charleston, and I start again. Whatever that lady thinks you did, you have to remember all the people you've helped, all the good you've done."

"It'll never be enough." He stared at her, his eyes bleak. "I so obviously ruined her life, and I have no idea who that woman was."

Malina sucked in a quick breath. Her belief in him faltered, then solidified even more strongly. Whatever injustice, real or imagined, Carr had caused, she didn't care. She'd insist he purge this toxin and forgive himself. *"Aberforth versus Bailey Industries.* Five years ago in Charleston."

Carr sighed. "I don't remember that one." He stared into his empty glass. "There are so many to pick from."

That's it. Malina plucked the tumbler from his hand, set it aside and dragged him to the sofa. There, she kept a tight hold on his hand, even though it hung limp and lifeless. "Spill it. So many what?"

"People I've destroyed."

"Oh, cut it out. You're not in a daytime melo-drama."

His head snapped up. "You don't know what I've done."

She much preferred the temper to the hopelessness. "You just said you don't remember either. How can you blame yourself for something you can't even recall?"

"I don't have to know specifics. Don't want to." He pulled away from her and rose. "I need you to go now."

Her heart contracted. "Carr, I—"

"Please. You need some rest, and I need to be alone for a while."

She'd never been good at comforting people. She had few friends and certainly hadn't inherited her mother's compassion. She was terrible with victims, since her instinct was to tell them the truth—your life's going to suck for a long time, and nothing I say is going to change that.

Apparently her abilities were just as poor with lovers. "Fine," she said as she stood and buttoned her jacket. "But no more booze."

Listless again, he shrugged. "Yeah. Sure."

She stepped close and laid her palm against his jaw. "I don't care what you've done in the past. I care about who you are now."

Then she kissed him and left.

In the car, she called Andrea. After arranging to meet her at the jewelry store the next morning, Malina told her about what had happened with Carr and asked his friend to check in on him later.

"What happened in this woman's case?" Andrea asked, her tone full of worry.

"I don't know, but I'm damn sure gonna find out."

MONDAY MORNING, Malina walked into a slightly shabby jewelry store on the edge of a respectable neighborhood in downtown Charleston.

She found Andrea Landry already inside the small, dark place, talking to an elderly man in a baby-blue cardigan. He held a jeweler's loupe up to one eye. He looked like somebody's birdhouse-making grandfather.

This case got weirder all the time.

"Malina," Andrea began with a twinkle in her eyes, "meet Bill Billings."

I rest my case.

Malina shook Billings's hand, then wasted no time in pulling the evidence bag from her jacket and handing over both the diamond and the list of stolen Australian gems.

Billings examined the stone, then, within moments, he was lowering his loupe and studying the list. "It's this one," he said, pointing at the seventh diamond on the list.

Malina exchanged a startled look with Andrea. "You're sure?"

"Gemology isn't an exact science, yet each gem is unique. Gems are identified by their weight, color and number and location of inclusions—naturally occurring flaws."

"Right," Malina said, nodding. "Like the fewer the imperfections, the more the stone's worth."

Billings smiled. "Exactly. If I was going to name the characteristics of this particular stone, this—" he pointed to the list "—is how I would catalog them. To be more certain, I'd need a microscope or a refractometer."

Malina angled her head. "A what?"

"It measures the refraction of light in a gem—the angles," Andrea explained. "I can get the diamond to someone who has one if you need."

"Yeah, that would be good." Malina directed her attention to Billings. "But you're reasonably confident even without this refractometer thing, right?"

"Hmm…reasonably confident," Billings said, as if testing both the idea and the words.

"As in, could you testify in a court of law regarding your findings if you were ever called on by the government to do so?"

"Court, huh?" He chuckled. "Sure, honey. Be glad to."

Malina returned the diamond to its envelope, thanked Billings for his time, then strode outside with Andrea.

"It looks like you found part of your Australian cache."

In the face of the bright sun overhead, Malina put on her sunglasses. "Looks like."

"So what's the next step?"

"Did you give me Bill Billings for fun, or does he really know what he's talking about?"

Andrea grinned. "Both."

"Thanks, I needed a laugh today." Malina shook her head ruefully. "People do some crazy-ass things to their kids."

"Don't they? He's got brothers named Will and Phil, if you can believe it."

"Absolutely bonkers."

Andrea shifted from one foot to the other. "Are you going to ask me about Carr?"

"He sent me home to get some sleep, and I didn't close my eyes all night." Malina sighed, exhausted and beyond worried. She was scared. About Carr's reaction to that unstable woman's assault, about the information she'd learned and about how much she cared concerning both. "Do you have time for some coffee?"

Andrea linked her arm through Malina's. "There's a shop two blocks over."

Tucked into a corner booth with caramel mocha lattes—way too sweet, but Malina hadn't wanted to be shrill and ask for plain coffee—they sipped and watched shoppers pass by the window for a couple of minutes before Andrea broke the silence.

"I've never seen him like that."

The guilt Malina had been battling back all night washed over her anew. "I shouldn't have left him." She bowed her head, massaging her temples. "I didn't know what to do. I've *never* not known what to do."

Andrea gripped her hand and squeezed. "It's harder to react when you care so much about the one in pain."

Malina managed to nod. Keeping the professional and personal separate. That had been her plan. What a joke.

"Do you want to hear it all?"

Malina lifted her head to stare into Andrea's understanding eyes. "I have to."

"I called him and asked if I could do anything. He blew me off, but I brought him dinner around six anyway. He refused to eat."

"Was he drinking?"

"No. Given his state, I was sort of surprised he was stone sober."

"He threw back a whiskey at three in the afternoon. I asked him not to have any more."

"Well, despite the pain he was in, he kept that promise."

"That's something, I guess."

Andrea glanced out the window before looking back at Malina's face. "I think he was punishing himself by not drinking. He was forcing himself to face what he'd done without anesthesia, as if he deserved to suffer."

So many what? she'd asked.

People I've destroyed, he'd answered.

"Yeah." Malina sipped the overly sweet coffee to burn away the emotions clogging her throat. "I can see that."

"When I refused to leave him, he stormed outside onto the beach."

"He likes to walk to relax," Malina mused, curling her hands into fists.

"I sent Tyler out to talk to him, but they nearly came to blows, so we pretended to go."

"Pretended?"

"Tyler and I waited until he'd set the house alarm and gone upstairs, then we spent the night on his sofa. We have each other's alarm codes in case there's an emergency while one of us is traveling."

Never before had Malina felt so powerless, ashamed and yet so grateful at the same time. "Thank you. I should have been there. He needed me, and I ran."

"Maybe so, but I think you're the one person he doesn't want to see. He doesn't want to face you. Why? Because of something in his past? Because some nutty woman clocked him?"

Malina shifted her gaze to Andrea's. "Did he say anything about her?"

"No. The only thing I got out of him was *he died because of my greed.* Do you know what he meant?"

"I do."

And she realized she and Carr had followed similar paths last night, though they'd been miles apart physically. He must have looked up the case he couldn't recall, just as she'd done.

So she told Andrea about *Aberforth versus Bailey Industries*.

Bailey manufactured kids' toys, mostly cheap, plastic wagons and indoor riding scooters for toddlers. Sandra Aberforth had tripped over her son's scooter and broken her hip. She'd had several surgeries, but would still walk with a slight limp the rest of her life. She was pissed and on the verge of bankruptcy, so she sued.

The court found in her favor and awarded her an astounding ten million dollars. Bailey Industries went belly-up six months later, and Charles Bailey killed himself a month after that.

The newspaper accounts of the trial credited the plaintiff attorney's impassioned closing statement with the unusually high judgment.

"Carr was the attorney," Andrea said, her eyes full of bleak understanding.

"I think we can assume the widow, Coraline Bailey, was the woman in the plum suit with the swift backhand." Malina cupped her hands around her coffee cup, hoping for warmth that didn't come. "She took up tennis and a crusade for tort reform after her husband's tragic death."

As awful as the case sounded in black and white, did the knowledge really change Malina's opinion of Carr? She wasn't naive. She'd always known a lawyer didn't get to his level of success without working a lot of different angles, cultivating a wily personality and pushing the boundaries of right and wrong. Saturday night she'd even teased him about owning lots of gray suits.

She hadn't cared then, when she was using his clever brain to help her solve her case. She had absolutely no right to judge him now.

And she found talking with Andrea made her understand the desire she had for him was as strong as ever. How many deals had the Bureau made with low-level criminals in order to get the guy at the top? How many times had she swallowed her personal opinions and followed orders she thought either overenthusiastic or impotent?

Justice wasn't always pretty.

As Carr had once told her, honesty and truth were two different concepts. So, whatever he'd done, whatever the lingering consequences of his actions, at some point he'd decided...

"That's why he defends churches and charities," Malina found herself saying aloud.

Andrea sipped her coffee. "Carr does work pretty closely with Sister Mary Katherine. They're an odd pair in a way, but—"

Malina grabbed Andrea by her wrist. "He's trying to make up for all the things he's done in his past. From the beginning, I thought his interest in the possibility of smuggling was too much. I could never figure out why he wanted to devote so much of his time to this case."

"Oh, come on. I think you probably had something to do with that."

"It's not just about me." Though Malina acknowledged that their desire was powerful, maybe even life-changing—at least for her. "He's repenting."

"Repenting?" Andrea flicked her hand to the side as she leaned back in the booth. "That's a bit dramatic."

"But he believes it," Malina insisted, hunching forward. "Absolutely."

For a few minutes, Andrea said nothing. Then, "Well, he *is* Catholic."

CARR FLUNG open his front door only after the patently annoying person on the porch apparently didn't get the message that he didn't want to be disturbed. Didn't a man have the right to refuse company anymore?

He was going to make damn sure that piece of legislation was on the next senate bill.

"Look, I don't—" He stopped, clenching his fist by his side.

Malina was on his porch. She was wearing the familiarly staid navy-blue suit, white shirt, sidearm and fierce expression.

He nearly fell to his knees.

"You don't want to see me?" she asked, her gaze and tone challenging. She grabbed his hand and tugged him outside, where the sun blared down on him. "Too bad."

He dug in his heels. He outweighed her, was certainly stronger physically. "I'm sick."

"So I noticed." She jerked him forward a few more steps, belying his confidence in his power. "Your secretary was helpful in telling me you haven't failed to show up at the office a single weekday in two years."

"Everybody's entitled to a day off."

"But not you. You're on a mission."

Despite his reluctance to leave, he found himself standing next to her sedan. "I'm sick."

"Bull." She pushed her face near his. "You're not a wallower, Hamilton. You're strong and crafty and determined. Sure, you've got issues. Don't we all?" She flung open the passenger door and pushed him inside. "Me, I'm terrified by you and what we become when we're together, but here I am anyway."

Slamming the door closed, she rounded the car with resolute strides, giving Carr his first hint of hope since yesterday. He'd been so sure she'd run from him after learning the ugly truth about his past.

There was no way she hadn't gone home and researched the case Mrs. Bailey had shoved in their faces. And still she was here.

Despite her need to get ahead and her desire to push at the strictures of justice, she'd never gone outside that barrier. He had. So many times.

And yet she was here; she hadn't turned away.

He wasn't sure whether to be grateful or angry. "Where're we going?"

"The shooting range."

Disbelieving, he stared at her profile. "The—"

She threw the car into Reverse, did a quick turn, then shot out onto the road. "You like to walk on the beach. I like to shoot. Let's try my way this time."

10

BEFORE CARR COULD blink, he found himself standing in an indoor shooting stall with a pistol in his hand and a target in the distance.

He felt ridiculous. How was this supposed to help him deal with the fact that he'd spent most of his life as an unconscionable leech?

With a sigh, he fired. Again. Then again.

Each time, the kick from the pistol jolted him back, and he found himself wanting to overpower the urge to recoil.

Malina laid her hand on his back and shouted over the other shots echoing through the range. "Relax your fingers! Keep your shoulders and stance strong."

Taking her advice, he found his rhythm smoother, his shots more accurate. At some point, the world around him fell away and all he saw was the target.

When the clip was empty, she reloaded for him, and he set off again.

He pictured nights he'd toasted victory with colleagues in Manhattan. He remembered the cold satisfaction he'd felt the first time one of his clients had received a judgment that was way out of proportion with the damage done. He recalled the times he'd smiled over companies driven to their knees or out of business entirely as a result of cases.

At the end of the fourth round, he was exhausted and oddly cleansed. The exercise had been brutal but absolutely necessary.

He and Malina might be different in many ways but she understood, as no one else could, that he needed a safe way to expend his anger. He'd spent the past few years hating himself, and he needed to kill his old life before he could truly move ahead to the new future he was embracing.

Not a therapy the good Sister might advocate, but one he supported anyway.

"Don't even think about doing that in reality," Malina said, snagging the gun from his hand and holstering it.

"Why?" He pulled off his headphones. "I didn't do so bad."

She glanced back at the target and winced. "Firearms are for trained professionals, which you most certainly are not."

He'd hit, well…something most of the time. "You do it," he challenged.

"Nah. Too easy."

"But you come here a lot."

Her gaze searched his, and whatever she found had her turning. "Come on."

After a walk down the hall, through a door and yet another hall, he found himself in a stark room with dark walls extending in a box in front of him. Malina walked to the far end of the room, where a computer rested.

She tapped the keys, then pulled a pistol, not from her holster, but a bin beside the monitor.

As she approached him, he noticed both the challenge in her eyes and the gun in her hand.

"It has the same weight as a real pistol," she said, shoving not an ammunition clip but a tiny card, like the ones in digital cameras, into the butt of the gun. "Ready?"

After a mesmerizing pause as he was captured senseless by her turquoise eyes, he nodded.

She pressed another button on a tiny black box against the wall.

The simulation began.

It was sort of like shooting ducks with a rifle at the fair, only the scene was a computer-generated, 3-D, all-too-real video game. The bad guys jumped out from all angles, firing at will. People screamed. The report of guns ricocheted. And, near the end, the lights went out and Carr heard random fire from seemingly all directions.

Malina simply closed her eyes and continued to knock off targets.

"How'd you do that?" Carr asked as they walked out of the gun club a while later.

"Arrange for you to shoot inanimate objects and save yourself thousands of dollars in therapy? I called and made a reservation."

"I got that." Carr slid his arm around her waist as he steered her back against the car. "How can you close your eyes and still hit all the targets?"

"I practice."

"Uh-huh." He pressed his body the length of hers, and she let out a quiet moan. He was alive again, and she was the reason. He skimmed kisses along her neck. "How?"

"You're certainly back to normal."

"Thanks to you. How?"

She met his gaze. "Your vision isn't as acute as your hearing in the dark. Closing my eyes helps me to focus. What you hear is just as important as what you see."

"Mmm…and what do you hear?" he whispered in her ear.

"You. I hear you…constantly." She wrapped her arms around his waist and laid her head against his chest.

The helplessness that had invaded him so thoroughly had lifted, and he knew both Malina's unusual brand of therapy, as well as the woman herself, had caused the change. What he didn't know was why she'd decided to help him.

She seemed to use any excuse to discount or outright avoid their relationship, and yet she was beside him. Holding him.

"How about dinner? I'm fairly certain there's a roasted chicken with vegetables in my fridge that's completely untouched."

"You're on."

THEY MANAGED idle conversation during dinner, but the moment the last plate was in the dishwasher, they grabbed each other.

Covering her mouth with his, he backed her against the kitchen counter as she attacked the buttons on his shirt. He cupped her cheek in his palm, angling her head, deepening the kiss with needy desperation. He slid his tongue against hers as they continued to fumble with their clothing, their fingers clumsy in desperation.

She got his pants and shirt unfastened, then rolled

a condom in place. He got her shirt off, her front-clasp bra unhooked and her pants and panties off. Just enough access so that when he lifted her onto the counter, he was able to enter her in one, smooth, deep stroke.

"Oh, man," she moaned. "Please do that again."

He obliged her until she'd wrapped her legs like a vise around his waist and her breathing grew choppy, frantic. She came on a hot groan of surrender, squeezing with potent, seductive pulses, bringing him to his own breath-stealing climax.

She collapsed against him. "I feel so much better."

He chuckled, stroking the silky length of her hair. "Hey, I was the one suffering."

She placed a kiss against his heaving chest. "Not the only one," she said so softly he could barely discern the words.

"Why are you here?" he asked reluctantly, not sure he could have if she'd been looking at him with those intense ocean eyes. "You don't want to be with me. Why should you?"

She clutched him tighter, with both arms and legs. "But I do."

Closing his eyes, he kissed the top of her head. He had no idea where they were headed, but he knew the journey was one he couldn't miss. "I never knew about Bailey's suicide until last night."

"I know."

"And you think that makes me better?"

"It makes you human."

"There are dozens, maybe hundreds out there like her. You've done a background check on me. You know what I was."

She finally lifted her head to look at him. "I know

you're a great attorney. You've won hundreds of judgments for your clients."

"And I never cared about one of them," he said harshly, turning away and fastening his pants. "I smiled at them, wined and dined them to get their lucrative cases, then I cashed my checks and never gave them another thought. I didn't take on small cases, ones with true injustice done."

She walked around him, still wearing only her unbuttoned shirt, unashamed in her nudity.

But then, she wasn't the one exposing her humiliating past.

"So you decided to make it your mission to beat yourself," she said. "That's why you defend churches, charities, anybody who's weak, underfunded or just has a righteous cause. You didn't want somebody like you coming along to subvert justice." She studied him as if seeing him for the first time. "Why? What changed?"

He grabbed her hand like a lifeline. "Come on. I'll tell you."

They settled on the sofa in the living room, and though she said she wasn't cold, he certainly was, so he settled at one end, tucking her back between his legs and a blanket on top of them both.

"My uncle died," he said into the silence. "If he hadn't..." He shook his head humbly. "Well, I might still be a shark with no soul or conscience."

She said nothing, simply rubbed her hands over his, where they rested against her stomach.

Who would have believed tough, decisive, my-way-or-the-highway Malina Blair's well of compassion was so deep and strong.

In that moment, he knew he loved her.

However illogical or ill-fated, she was the one he'd been searching for, hoping and praying for.

He leaned his face into her hair, breathing in the clean scent, wanting to remember her long after she left him for bigger and better things in Washington. In many ways, it was right that he should love but not have.

"He was an attorney in New York, too," he continued. No secrets could be held between him and this woman now. He couldn't protect his heart anymore, after all. "He was my mentor and had a lucrative practice in products liability. He taught me the ropes, sponsored me at his country club in the Hamptons, introduced me to fine wines and beautiful women.

"Other than my years at Yale, I'd spent my life on Palmer's Island, and I was dazzled by all of it."

Carr forced himself to look back and remember expensive dinners, flashy nightclubs and meaningless nights with vapid women who couldn't care less how he paid the bills, as long as he did.

"I learned the game quickly," he continued. "I helped us expand to environmental disasters and class action suits. And the money rolled in.…"

"Okay, stop." Malina held up her hand and twisted around to glare at him. "A lot of those companies deserved judgments against them. I read your file. Chemical spills. People with chronic pain and cancer. Blatant plant safety violations. You aren't the only villain here."

"You think I'm a villain?"

She looked exasperated. "You seem determined to cast yourself in that role. I was merely helping."

When she settled back against him, he continued. "We took only cases that were capable of bringing in big judgments. I protested that policy at first, then as I made more money and our firm's reputation rose higher and higher, I bought my luxury uptown apartment and didn't much care how I'd arrived there.

"I'd sold out. I knew it when it was happening and chose to ignore the warnings my conscience tried to occasionally instill. I used my brains and charm without scruples, and I became a huge success."

Malina clutched his fingers, as if she was afraid of the scene he described.

"Only my uncle's sudden heart attack jolted me back to reality, made me face what I'd become. I swore I wouldn't die as he had—rich, bitter, unconscionable and alone. So, I closed the practice, packed up and came home."

She turned. "That's it? You didn't kick kids or dogs or homeless people?"

"Kick—" What was she talking about? "No, of course not."

She laid her hands against his cheeks. "I have a thing for dogs—golden retrievers in particular, and I don't care about the rest of it. I didn't know you then, and the man in front of me now is the one I'm interested in."

The look in her eyes was steady, unyielding and vividly blue. She should be running from him, and she wasn't.

Grateful beyond words, he leaned forward and kissed her.

She returned his touch ardently, straddling his lap and parting his shirt, then pushing it off his shoulders. Within moments, they were naked and she was beneath him, moaning his name, giving him solace and understanding with strokes instead of words.

As they lay on their sides, satisfied and replete, he continued to slide his hands up and down her warm, bare back. He wanted to say things, pretty words that spoke to the depths of his emotions. But he knew she wasn't ready to hear them, and he wanted to hear her rejection even less.

Pushing her tangled hair off her face, he brushed his lips across her cheek. "Would you be so understanding if someone else, not me, admitted they'd done all those things?"

She winced. "Probably not." When he grinned, she asked, "How is that a *good* thing?"

"It makes me special."

She rolled her eyes, but she was clearly holding back a smile.

"Let's do my favorite thing now," he said.

"I thought we just did."

He slapped her backside lightly. "I meant walk on the beach."

WEARING HER NAVY SLACKS, which would never be the same after the salt water dried on them, and one of Carr's old Yale sweatshirts, Malina kicked through the cold surf. "Chicken," she said when he jumped out of reach of the spraying water.

He stretched out his arm and grabbed her hand, dragging her onto firmer, drier sand. "If you want a swim, the pool's heated."

"I didn't bring my suit."

Pulling her against his side, the expression on his face became decidedly lecherous. "That won't be a problem."

She drank in the hungry look in his dark eyes. He did have a way of making her heart race and her knees weak. "I'll bet."

"After we walk, okay?"

She nodded mutely. Falling under Carr's potent spell was like falling asleep, fast and natural. It was no wonder the man had made millions off juries.

Hand in hand, they continued walking down the beach, which was surprisingly peaceful. Malina only had the urge to take off in a sprint once. It wasn't 3-D hostage takeover simulations, but it wasn't half-bad.

"So how did things go with the jeweler this morning?" he asked.

Oh, right. She was here only long enough to solve a boatload of cases so she could hightail it back to D.C.

And why did that suddenly seem like a lousy plan? Why did part of her long to walk with Carr up and down this tiny stretch of beach in the middle of nowhere for years on end?

But was she really considering giving up her career dreams for a man? Didn't she want to move up the Bureau's elite ladder? Didn't she want to make Director?

Shaking aside her internal questions, she recounted her and Andrea's encounter with Bill Billings, finding it hard to believe that had only occurred this morning.

"So Simon, Jack, plus associates really did steal diamonds from that mine in Australia and bring them to South Carolina to unload."

"Sure looks that way."

"I actually stumbled onto an international jewel theft ring."

That would certainly go to his head. "Yep."

Carr stopped suddenly. "And we have absolutely no proof."

"We've got a stolen diamond."

"Found on a public dock with no fingerprints or any other forensic evidence."

"We witnessed Jack carrying a box on the dock just before we found the diamond."

"But we didn't see the diamond fall out of the box. Theoretically, it could have already been there."

"You witnessed an exchange of merchandise for money between Jack and his cronies."

Looking wildly frustrated, Carr kicked sand with his foot. "They could have been buying and selling candlesticks, baseball caps, shells from the seashore."

"Shells from the seashore?" Malina repeated. "Do you ever stop being a lawyer?"

"No, it's instinctive—like you and your little gun games. And it's a good thing for you that my instincts are finely honed. We know what happened, we know pretty much everybody involved in the crime, but we've got nothing to prove it in court."

"We have Simon and his varied aliases."

Carr waved that away. "From prints obtained illegally. It's not enough."

"No, it isn't."

"You don't seem worked up about that little reality." When she shrugged, he seemed to finally realize her calm had a reason. "You've got a plan."

"I've got some definite ideas."

Laughing, he grabbed her and swung her into his arms, heading back toward the house. "All in all, I usually like your ideas."

"Usually?"

"I seem to recall you ordering me off your case several times."

"Even the best agents can make mistakes."

"You admit making a mistake? Remind me to note this date and time in my PDF."

Part of her wanted to tell him to put her down, she

could walk herself. But the house's landscape lights glowed in the distance, accenting its round, modern features, and Malina sighed against his shoulder instead.

She was pretty crazy about that house.

Promising they'd talk through her ideas after their swim, Carr set her down by the pool. She was in the process of, yet again, unbuttoning his shirt—really, the man should just walk around bare chested—when she noticed movement from inside his house.

Cursing the carelessness that had her leaving her Glock on the kitchen counter, she stepped between him and the windows. "Get down."

"Wha—"

She grabbed his arm and jerked him to a crouch. "Be quiet. Stay here."

Careful to keep to the shadows, she inched closer to the windows. Carr, naturally, ignored her order and followed.

"This is Palmer's Island," he whispered when they stopped behind a shrub underneath the kitchen window. "I leave my doors unlocked all the time. It's probably just some lost tourist."

Malina looked at him in disbelief. "This is Palmer's Island, home to an international jewel theft ring."

"Hmm, good point. Still, you did that yesterday with Mrs. Bailey—jumped between me and her. I can handle myself, you know."

"Whatever."

"Do you really think Jack or Simon is on to us?"

"Obviously I didn't, since my pistol is inside."

"Are you always this cranky during missions?"

"Are you always this chatty?"

She needed to know what they were facing so she could decide if they should head for the car or if they could handle whoever they'd encounter inside. She risked a peek at the corner of the window.

After a quick glance, she sighed and dropped next to Carr. "You can handle yourself, huh? How about a nun sitting at your kitchen table?"

11

"THANK YOU so much, Carr," Sister Mary Katherine said as she accepted a china teacup and saucer. "I'm sure this will warm me right up."

Malina kept her distance. She felt as if her usual control had flown the coop on angel's wings. Andrea had confided all about the case to the good Sister, which was enough to make Malina grind her teeth, but she also found herself hanging on to her edgy mood at being caught unaware and unarmed.

"Surely you don't think you'll need that, Agent Blair."

Malina jerked her hand back from her holstered pistol, which she'd been about to put on. "Of course not," she said, facing the smiling nun. "Sorry. It's an instinct when I'm working."

Carr moved behind her, laying his hands on her shoulders and rubbing lightly, as if he knew how tense she felt. "We thought you were intruders when we first saw you through the window."

"It's no wonder," Andrea said, sitting beside the Sister with her own cup of tea. "The front door was unlocked.

Really, Carr. There are jewel thieves running around the island."

With a significant look, Malina glanced back at her lover and felt much, much better.

"You didn't come to church yesterday," the Sister began, her tone holding just the right amount of accusation. "I couldn't reach you on your phone all afternoon, and when I dropped by this evening, there was no answer at your door. I became concerned and went to Andrea's."

"She was convinced something horrible had happened to you," Andrea said, picking up the story. "Given yesterday's events…" She glanced briefly at Malina. "Well, I felt it was best we come check."

Carr cleared his throat. "I'm sorry to have worried you ladies. We just went for a walk on the beach."

"He got over his virus pretty quickly," Malina added, proud she could keep a straight face. "Nothing some TLC couldn't cure."

Andrea's lips twitched. "I'm so glad to hear it."

"I think I'll have some wine." Malina patted his hand. "Carr?"

"Love some. In fact, I'll help you open it." He was right behind her as she opened the fridge. "Okay, so this is all my fault," he whispered in her ear. "I was looking forward to a swim, too, you know."

Malina pulled a bottle of Pinot Grigio from the fridge. As she set the bottle on the counter, Carr handed her a corkscrew. "Did Andrea have to spill about the thefts? I didn't really have a role for a nun in my plans."

"She probably did. The Sister can be pretty persuasive."

"How quickly can we get rid of them?"

"The Sister will expect us to tell her how we're going to stop these guys."

"I thought Tyler was the sheriff."

"Sure he is."

Malina poured out two glasses of wine, then tapped hers against Carr's. "Fine. I'll bring her in." She met his gaze. "On a consultant basis only."

"We could always send her over to the SAC—that would keep her occupied."

"I'd like to actually keep my job, if you don't mind." Glancing at the Sister, Malina sipped the crisp wine. "She's kind of cute, though."

"Malina, no kidding, you can't underestimate her."

"Fear, huh?" She shifted her gaze to his, then grabbed him by the collar of his shirt and jerked him toward her. "Makes me want to be naughty."

"You've lost your mind." Still, as she nibbled at his lips, he pressed himself against her.

"No, I just feel like breaking the rules a little."

"Agent Blair," the Sister said quietly, making Carr's body jolt. "I'd very much like to hear how you're going to rid this island of its most recent criminal element."

"Yes, ma'am," Malina said, releasing Carr and reluctantly dragging her gaze away from the sexy need in his eyes. "I've got some definite ideas on how I want to handle things."

Carr groaned in her ear, stroked his hand discreetly down her backside, then they headed toward the kitchen table.

Everybody sat but Malina, who preferred to stand and occasionally pace.

She wished the sheriff could have been present, since she admired Tyler's decisiveness and she'd need him to help keep an eye on their suspects before she launched her plan. But he'd been called to duty for a case of teenage vandalism—the local high school baseball team had stolen the rival school's pig mascot—and he had to work the interrogation before the co-conspirators—the cheerleaders—followed through on the threat to have a beach barbecue.

"My idea is relatively simple," Malina began. "Though it requires lots of bad cops and one good one." At this, she looked to Carr. He was as good as they came. And in a variety of ways.

"We confront Jack with the diamond—actually a simulated one, since the real one is on its way to Andrea's expert for analysis. I'm hoping you and your pal Billings can help with the fake, Andrea."

"Of course," she said. "We can come up with something."

Malina stared out the window, but she could see the scenario in her mind as clearly as the people in front of her. She could only hope the reality would be as effective. "We go at Jack hard and fast, busting into the office in the middle of the day, shouting about who we are, who we want, with guns drawn, Kevlar vests on every agent—the works."

"This sounds very violent," Sister Mary Katherine said, clearly wary.

"It won't be." Malina turned from the window and faced the delicate-looking nun, who probably had more spine than half the Bureau. "It's the shock of the moment that'll spook Jack Rafton. He thinks he wants to be a bad guy, but he's really only after the cash and the excitement."

"And the hot cars," Carr added.

Sister Mary Katherine nodded. "He's a lost soul."

Malina shrugged. "If you like. We interrogate Rafton at his office and pray he doesn't ask for an attorney."

"And if he does?" Carr asked.

"Then we're screw—um, out of luck. But I don't think he will at first. He'll think he can talk his way out of anything. So I push him—we know what you're up to, we know about the robbery, you'll be charged with an international felony. The Australian government, Interpol, the FBI, etc. We all want you.

"When I've got him on the ropes, then you come in, Carr." She shifted her attention directly to him. "You have to be careful not to agree to be his attorney—you don't do criminal cases, but maybe you could recommend a friend. You're just there to hold his hand."

"My favorite role," Carr returned, setting his wineglass on the table with a snap.

"But it's a critical one," Andrea said before Malina could. "You'll be his lifeline among the chaos. He'll relax and tell Malina what she needs to know." Andrea looked at Malina. "That's the goal, right? To get him to roll over on Simon."

Grateful for Andrea's support, but worried about Carr's strained expression, Malina nevertheless nodded. "That's the only chance we've got."

Carr said nothing for several minutes. He stared at the stem of his wineglass, which he turned round and round on the kitchen table. "It skirts the line of an attorney's role and allegiance. By standing with Jack, I'm implying I'm on his side."

Malina had been worried about this obstacle. After Carr's recent confessions, she didn't think he'd particularly like her tactics. But the plan had been brewing ever since she'd met Simon, or whoever he really was. He was the kind who used weaker people, over and over, while he slipped away like a snake in the night. She wanted him behind bars and his pretend lifestyle of respectability exposed.

Carr's problem was that he saw too much of himself in Jack and Simon. He saw himself as the villain. Malina was going to make it her personal mission to prove him wrong—to prove that though his decisions had caused heartache in some, his talents had changed the lives of others.

He may not have intended to do good, but he had.

"Would you rather the thieves get away with their crimes?" Malina challenged. "Maybe they'll think Palmer's Island is a nice, quiet place to set up shop permanently?"

Carr scowled at her, then directed his attention to the nun. "Sister Mary Katherine?"

Regally, the Sister nodded, then her steadfast gaze moved to Malina and held. "Do you often feel forced to lie during the course of investigating your cases, Agent Blair?"

"No," Malina said coolly. "I lie by choice in order to put people behind bars, people who corrupt and taint the lives of ordinary citizens who simply want to live free and happy. Do you have a problem with that?"

The nun blinked, probably not used to people who met her challenges head-on. But Malina believed in degrees of right and wrong, and intention was a critical element. She hoped the good Sister had some sense of that philosophy.

Finally, she linked her pale, vein-covered hands in front of her on the table. "I certainly don't. Do you think Carr is essential to your capture of these men?"

"Yes. Without him there, I'm the enemy, and he'll

clam up and hire a guy who'll tell him to keep his mouth shut while the lawyers haggle the details for days."

Andrea sighed. "And the real thief—Simon Ellerby— slips quietly away."

Malina had no intention of letting that happen, but she knew it was a possibility. "Exactly."

"Do you want to do this, Carr?" the Sister asked him.

You decided to make it your mission to beat yourself. You didn't want somebody like you coming along to subvert justice.

Malina could all but see her words from earlier zipping through his brain.

"Very much," he said.

"Then I think you should," the Sister concurred.

Carr absorbed this verdict with a nod. "Is this the plan the SAC would recommend?" he asked Malina.

"Hel—" Glancing at the nun, Malina cleared her throat. "No, I don't think so. He'd recommend watching the suspects a while longer, seeing if we can find out more about all the members of the group. Jack might not be the most vulnerable link."

"But the diamonds are gone already," Andrea said. "Or nearly are."

Malina was really starting to like that woman, even if she didn't get the whole thieves-as-friends concept. "Exactly. We don't have the luxury of surveillance and research time."

"After we confront him, Jack could run," Carr warned, who seemed to be as committed to his role as devil's advocate. "Or, worse, rat us out to Simon."

"The minute he agrees to talk, I'll put him in protective custody."

Carr lifted his eyebrows. "Won't Simon be suspicious

if Jack suddenly disappears? And if the SAC doesn't approve, how are you going to get authorization for the deal?"

"The SAC will approve," Malina insisted. *I just have to do a better job selling this to him than I am to you.* "And we'll be watching Ellerby. Losing Jack will make him panic, do something stupid, then we'll have him."

We could always send her over to the SAC, Carr had said about Sister Mary Katherine. That wasn't a half-bad idea. But the *her* Malina wanted to send wasn't the nun, but Andrea. Her expertise and neutrality would go a long way to getting Sam to approve the operation.

"If he does, then fine, I'm in." Carr rose and faced Malina. "I have one suggested change."

"Naturally."

"Get Jack to make a call to Ellerby and set up a meeting between him and me. I'll get corroborating evidence out of him."

Malina had no doubt that he could, but it wasn't him she was worried about. Okay, maybe she was. There was no way Simon wasn't a smart, dangerous guy. He'd pulled off quite a few jobs over the years. Though most thieves weren't violent, most were into burglary, not major thefts. Simon Ellerby was a different animal. "Jack couldn't pull off a call like that," she said. "He'd panic."

"His very real panic is what will make the sting work," Carr insisted. "We get him to tell Simon that he wants out. He doesn't have the nerves for the business, so he broke down and blabbed about the thefts to a colleague—me. He sets up a meeting between me and Simon. During that meeting, I offer to take Jack's place." When Malina stubbornly shook her head, he added mockingly, "If he looks at my background, he'll easily believe I could fit right in with the gang."

Malina glared at him. He was going to use his past mistakes to close this case? More punishment and retribution?

She didn't like it. Not one bit.

She felt as if agreeing would be sacrificing her lover for her job. Something she'd have done a few months ago without question. Now, the whole idea made her sick.

"He's right, Malina," Andrea said, and Malina suddenly liked her less than before. "Jack's testimony against Simon may not be enough. And what if losing Jack doesn't spook Simon into doing something stupid?"

Carr nodded. "If I could get Simon to spill details about the operation, however…"

"I don't like it." And Malina liked even less the way her gut tightened. It wasn't just the idea of a civilian going undercover with a major case on the line. She didn't want her lover caught continually in a cycle of retribution. She didn't want him thinking it was his sole duty to right this wrong. She didn't want Carr within a hundred yards of Simon Ellerby.

Sister Mary Katherine pursed her lips. "This addition to the plan does seem a little dangerous. You will be careful, won't you, Carr?"

As CARR CLOSED the front door behind Andrea and Sister Mary Katherine, Malina rounded on him. "Were you trying to show your balls are bigger than mine or were you deliberately trying to piss me off?"

"Neither. My plan is better."

"You think a *nun* really understands the danger you'll

be in?" Malina stormed down the hall. "You think she has any idea that if you stumble over any word, phrase or gesture, Simon Ellerby could put a bullet in your head and dump you overboard from his cozy little yacht?"

Finding her anger oddly comforting, Carr followed her. "I thought you said most thieves aren't violent."

"He's not most thieves, and he'll probably have some weak-minded associate do the actual deed."

Much as that idea wasn't remotely appealing, Carr knew he had to do this. He'd dragged all of them into this mess. It was only right he be there to wrap it up. "I won't stumble."

Malina pointed at him. "Next case, Counselor, you're riding the bench."

He grabbed her by her wrist and pulled her into his arms. "Oh, so you think you'll be around beyond this case?"

"Sure. This whole thing is going to blow up in my face, and I'll be stuck here forever." She caught the spasm of hurt that crossed his face. "No offense. But nuns, neighbors with thieving friends and an idiotic insurance agent whose biggest goal in life is to be a criminal? I've lost my mind thinking this is going to work."

"You forgot the morally ambiguous attorney in your cast of characters."

She sent him a defiant stare. "You're not morally ambiguous."

Not anymore. He laid his cheek against the top of her head. The love he had for her was the reason he was fighting to get his life back. He hadn't started out knowing she was there to fight for, but now that he did, he finally understood the power of redemption.

"You shouldn't worry about me," he said. "I can

handle this. I'm an expert at charm and lies—in case you hadn't noticed."

Her toughness finally gave way, and Malina clutched him against her. "I don't want you to do it."

"But I need to do it."

"It's part of your punishment?"

"No. It's me using my talents for something good and true, something that matters." Her heart thumped against his chest, and he drew a bracing breath. She was everything. How could he not help her—and make up for the past a bit more in the process? *"He's after the cash and the excitement,* you said earlier. I was Jack Rafton."

"Oh, please. You've never been that weak and stupid."

"I need to do this."

She said nothing for a moment. Then, "I'm going with you to meet with Simon." When he frowned, she added, "You're an expert at charm and lies. You'll think of an excuse for me—or rather Sandy—to tag along. There's no way you're doing this without backup."

"I hadn't planned to, but I was thinking I'd wear a wire and you'd be listening in, ready to burst onto the scene, armed and dangerous, if things got dicey."

"I'll be with you, and a team of agents will be ready to burst onto the scene."

"Fine," he said, though the idea that she would also be in danger didn't exactly thrill him.

Her job, however, involved considerable risk, and if he wanted to be with her, he was going to have to get used to that idea.

"Oh, good. We're even. How about a swim to burn off that tension?"

His whole body went hard. "You fight dirty."

She slid her cheek across his chest, then sank her teeth, ever so lightly, into his earlobe. "I know you're committed to the straight and narrow these days, but I bet you can remember how that works."

In answer, he swung her into his arms, strode out the back door and dumped her into the pool.

He knelt on the smooth stone deck as she popped to the surface, spitting water from her mouth and rubbing it from her eyes. "Come to think of it," he said, reaching out to stroke her cheek. "I do remember how to fight dirty."

Naturally, she jerked him in.

By the time he found his feet, she'd already shed her sopping clothes and was plowing through the water making laps.

Naturally, he chased her.

He caught her and dragged her to the shallow end next to the waterfall that flowed over the rock formation that was part of the pool area landscaping.

Their verbal battle had heightened his need, which he'd once considered impossible with Malina. In addition, a bone-deep fear of the upcoming plan had settled into his bones. Logically, he knew she could handle herself, but love wasn't reasonable.

Caging her against the side of the pool, he moved his mouth over her slick skin, glorying in the way she clutched him against her body. She angled her head, giving him better access to the delicate skin between her neck and shoulders.

With her help, he managed to peel off his clothes. Thankfully, the vacuum-packed condoms had fared better than his pants and shirt.

He teased her, pressing at the entrance of her body,

and she moaned, grasping his hips. How long she'd need him was uncertain, but all he had was the moment.

Knowing he couldn't hold her forever, he pushed inside her, and she gasped, meeting his rhythm, and the panic of losing her burst through him with sudden intensity. Why couldn't this go on? Why couldn't she stay?

Why wouldn't she love him?

Her body tensed, and he forced his dread aside. He sought only pleasure now—hers and his.

What else did he have?

"YOU DON'T trust your own judgment anymore?" Malina asked him as they sat, wrapped in a blanket, on the sofa beside the outdoor fireplace a while later. "You have to ask the Sister?"

He kissed her temple, breathing in the clean, refreshing scent of her hair. "Not in some cases."

"I think that's stupid."

Leave it to Malina to not hold back. "It's not."

She craned her neck around to stare at him. "I'm also not crazy about you confronting Simon."

"I've been there from the beginning—even before you arrived, by the way. You won't deny me the reward of seeing this through to the end."

"You're not a trained agent. You could get hurt."

Smiling, he asked. "Worried about me?"

"Yes."

"I can handle myself."

"Doesn't mean there's not a risk."

He stroked her cheek, taking great pleasure from the concerned look in her eyes. "I need this, Malina. You know I do."

"Fine," she said, turning back toward the fire.

"Are your parents proud of you?"

She glanced briefly. "That's some segue."

"Sorry. I'm a little rough around the edges lately." As happy as she made him, in some ways he felt as if his life were falling apart, bit by bit, and while he recognized what was happening, he had no way to stop its progression. "Are they?"

"I guess. Yes," she admitted, somewhat reluctantly it seemed. "They don't really understand why I do what I do, but they support me."

"What do they do?"

"They run a surf shop."

For some reason, that made him smile. He'd imagined Malina with stern, exacting parents. "No kidding?"

"My mom paints, too. I've tried to get her showings in a gallery in Honolulu, but she doesn't think anybody would be interested in her work."

"So, she's…"

"The complete opposite of me, yes. She has zero ambition beyond keeping a leaky roof over her head. She wouldn't know a pistol from a crossbow, or a con man from a tourist in flowered shorts. Who are sometimes the same person," she added drily.

The exasperated affection in her voice was so normal, so lovely, so completely different from his feelings about his own parents, it made Carr's smile broaden.

"They wanted more kids," she continued, "but it never happened for them. These days, they bring in foster kids, which, on Kauai, usually turn out to be lost college students on spring break. Are your parents proud of you?"

"I have absolutely no idea."

That had her turning her whole body around to face him.

Faced with that forceful gaze, he had a hard time pulling off a casual shrug. "They think I was crazy to leave Manhattan and come here."

"Didn't they raise you here?"

"No, my grandmother did. She passed away when I was in college."

"You weren't raised by your parents," she said slowly, as if needing clarification.

"They never planned to have a child. My mother had family money, so they've always moved around Europe and the Caribbean."

Pinched annoyance drew her brows together. "They abandoned you."

He kissed away the wrinkles. "I was better off, believe me. But genetics do tell occasionally, so I'm assuming that's where I get my selfishness."

"A soulless, money-grubbing uncle and idiotic, narcissistic parents. How'd you turn out so great?"

He leaned in, nibbling at her lips. "You think I'm great?"

She laid her hand in the center of his chest, pressing him back. "Seriously, that's a pretty sucky childhood."

"Was it? I grew up in paradise and was raised by a woman who loved me. I always had the beach, friends, and plenty of material things."

"But, essentially, you were alone."

"True. You were, too. Do you feel deprived?"

"No." She sighed. "Though there were moments of teenage rebellion and back talk that I'm sure my parents wouldn't be too anxious to revisit. We were talking about you."

"Actually, we initially began the discussion about you and whether or not your parents are proud of you. So we seem to have come full circle. Want to share some more childhood trauma?"

"Not really, no."

"You sure you don't want to talk about when you decided that bow marksmanship was preferable to waxing surfboards?"

"Look, Counselor, you're the one with damaged moral issues. And, can I add that you're a lot more forthcoming when we're having sex?"

He moved his lips across her feather-soft cheek. "Oh, that can be easily arranged."

She pressed her finger into his chest. "The question is, why did you bring it up?"

"Sex? I always—"

"No, your parents."

"Starved for conversation?"

"Ha! You're never at a loss for words, at least not until yesterday."

It was his turn to sigh. "I find myself having a hard time just now."

"Well, stop it."

"Okay." With that fierce blue gaze boring into his, how could he not? With her warmth so close and accessible, how could he let the past turn him cold?

"Though you're liable to use my words at some point to boost an ego that already seems inherently healthy, hear this, Carr Hamilton." She held him in her sights as surely as any target at the end of her pistol, and her voice was as hard and true as any bullet. "You're a good man. And though your parents may be idiots and your grandmother gone and your moral advisor a bit too committed to black and white, I need you. I've needed your help with this case. I've needed you to introduce me to your sort-of-law-abiding friends. And I've especially needed you to challenge me and remind me of what's at stake."

With that pronouncement, she wrapped her arms around him and hugged him tightly against her.

"Glad to be there," he managed to say gruffly into her hair.

The one person's approval he wanted, he had. What else was there?

The future would come, and choices would be made, but right now he had it all—the way he dreamed he might if he changed his life for the better.

"You're taking a big chance," he said a few minutes later, "moving on Jack like this."

"Sure, but my way is the only way, remember?" She leaned back and planted a firm kiss on his lips. "Besides, I'm tired of playing it safe. I may even wear a red suit."

12

"COME ON, Rafton." Malina spoke harshly, shaking her head as she stood in front of the terrified insurance agent. "We know you're in this up to your greedy, bloodshot eyeballs."

"I—" Jack Rafton cast a panicked glance around his office, where several armed FBI agents, sheriff's deputies and crime-scene techs were milling around, talking in low tones while they either studied him or gathered evidence in plastic bags and packed up all his computer equipment. "You're wrong."

"Judge North feels differently," Malina said, waving the search warrant.

"Y-you could be bluffing."

"Could be." Malina laid her hand deliberately on the butt of her gun. "But I'm not."

"But I—"

"Do you honestly think that I'd bring my team in here without cause? You think the Bureau is just sitting around, waiting to pounce on private businesses 'cause we got nothin' better to do? We have terrorists to hunt. And, yet, we came in here, armed and ready, bulletproof vests in place, because we know you've hooked up with some seriously bad dudes. We were ready to shoot if provoked." Malina lurched forward, bracing her hands on the desk chair where he sat. "Do you have plans to provoke me, Jack?"

"N-no."

"I understand you've got a nice island here, lovely vacation spot. How do you think your fellow citizens are going to feel when word gets out that you've brought these thieving scumbags to their shores?"

"Agent Blair," Carr said, his tone disappointed, "you said you'd keep this matter quiet."

"And I will." Never looking Carr's way, she sent Rafton a glare. "As long as I get what I want."

"B-but…" Rafton blustered. "I have rights. Don't I have rights, Carr?"

Carr laid his hand on the other man's shoulder and returned Malina's glare. "Of course you do."

"Please, Hamilton." Malina rolled her eyes, and though they'd agreed to this plan of action it still bothered her to see the hurt briefly cross Carr's face. "Don't give me any of that bleeding-heart crap."

Carr had offered moral support, not legal representation, but it was clear Rafton relied upon his judgment anyway. Malina had a team of agents watching Simon Ellerby to make sure he was on his yacht and wouldn't pop in to find one of his compatriots was being interrogated by the cops and thereby ruin the operation. Everything was moving along as they'd anticipated. If only they could drive Jack to the edge where he'd turn on his boss.…

"We know about the Lotus, Rafton." Malina shook her head as if disappointed. "Pretty reckless. Didn't you go to any of those helpful classes at the last Smugglers International Convention?"

"I'm not a smuggler!" he squeaked.

"Oh, yeah?" Malina pointed at the landscape painting on the wall beside his bookcases. "What's that?"

Rafton turned sheet-white, and Malina's heart jumped. It had been a wild stab, but after Carr's observations of the crates coming off the boat, plus Andrea's speculation that Rafton had to be passing over more than diamonds, Malina had begun to wonder just how long the list of stolen goods was liable to wind up being.

"Well, well," Malina chortled, pacing around him. "The gang's just floating in illicit merchandise."

"There's no gang," Rafton said desperately. "I didn't steal any diamonds—or paintings. I don't know what you're talking about."

"Be smart, Jack," Carr said in a low, soothing tone. "If any of this is true, your cooperation could go a long way to keeping you out of federal prison."

"Prison!" Rafton jerked to his feet. "You're out of your mind! I'm not going to prison."

Malina leaned back against the desk and made an effort to look bored. "Sure seems that way to me." She paused significantly. "But then it's not you we want."

"Who then?"

Approaching him, Malina stopped mere inches away. "Simon Ellerby."

Based on Rafton's reaction, she decided—though she'd already suspected—that the insurance agent would make a lousy poker player.

She angled her head. "Listen, Jack, you don't have the stones for this. You're drowning. And when we offer a deal to Ellerby, you can bet he'll jump on it and screw you to the wall."

Rafton drew his shoulders back. "I have no idea who you're talking about."

"You went to a party on his yacht last week," Carr interjected.

"No kidding?" Malina forced surprise. "Isn't that interesting? What exactly went on at this party?"

Rafton winced. "Carr, please."

Carr shrugged. "You can't pretend you don't know him, Jack. Lying to the federal authorities isn't going to help the situation."

They worked him for more than an hour, but he simply alternated between panic and denial.

He admitted nothing.

Malina took to clenching the butt of her pistol. Her finger twitched many times toward the trigger, and she silently recited federal penal codes as a way of distracting her from her instincts to break ninety-nine percent of those codes.

While Rafton bent his head, Carr, who stood just behind him, looked at Malina and lifted his eyebrows.

Time for the secret weapon.

Since she could hear the words as clearly as if he'd spoken them aloud, she scowled.

But what choice did she have? Moving quickly on Ellerby was essential.

She turned away from the two men and started out of the room. "Mr. Hamilton, get your friend a glass of water. I'll be back."

Outside in the bright sunshine, a brisk wind whipping off the Atlantic, Malina walked to her car, parked at the curb. The idea had come to Carr in the middle of the night—he'd literally woken Malina up out of a dead sleep to give her this last, fail-safe tactic.

If the dog-napping case had given her office ridicule, she couldn't wait to find out what humiliation this latest, unconventional strategy was going to bring.

As she opened the passenger side door, she noted the woman inside was knitting, gathering together strands of blue and green yarn from opposite sides of her lap. "We're going to need you."

Sister Mary Katherine glanced up, her expression calm as she nodded and set her yarn aside. "I anticipated as much. Jack was in Sister Agatha's Sunday studies during high school, and she assured me he was an attentive student."

"Yeah, he's a prince, all right," Malina said as she helped the nun out of the car.

Sister Mary Katherine pursed her lips. "The Church can redeem everyone who's lost, everyone willing to change their life."

"As Carr will undoubtedly attest."

"Are you angry with me, Agent Blair?" the Sister asked as they headed toward the office door.

"No. No, of course not," Malina added, barely suppressing a wince. She wasn't exactly religious, but she had great respect for those who willingly devoted their lives to the greater good. "I just—" She stopped and whirled to face the nun. "Carr's a good man." She flung her hand in the direction of the office. "He's not Jack Rafton or anyone in his gang. He tried to help people. Is he a criminal because he made a lot of money?"

The nun folded her hands in front of her. "No one said he was a criminal."

"But he thinks he is!" When a couple of guys who were hauling computer equipment from Rafton's office paused on the sidewalk, Malina ground down on her temper. "I don't appreciate you, or anybody else, putting him down."

"You are angry."

She was. At least part of her. She knew the good Sister wasn't the villain here, but she didn't appreciate anybody who didn't see Carr's need to help others. And she wasn't exactly sure where Sister Mary Katherine stood. "Do you know his parents abandoned him?"

"I do."

That wasn't a surprise really. It was a small island after all. But the sadness in the nun's eyes took Malina aback. Her vision of nuns was tough love and rulers smacking on knuckles. Clearly a stereotype that wasn't worthy of the woman before her.

How many times had Malina busted stereotypes of snipers and marksmen? *Ahem, women.*

Well, hell, she and the Sister had something in common.

Okay, maybe not hell, exactly.

"He's not morally ambiguous," Malina asserted, still uncertain where the Sister stood regarding Carr.

"Well, no." The Sister laid one hand over her heart. "He's the exact opposite. At least now. There was a time…"

Malina pressed her lips together to keep from shouting. "Do you honestly think the people he won cases for cared about his motives for helping them?"

"I have no idea. But *he* cares about his motives. Carr feels the need to make up for his past." Sister Mary Katherine held up her hand to forestall Malina's interruption. "Whether or not it's required by you, me or anyone else doesn't matter. This is something he's compelled to do."

"Something you encouraged him to do," Malina insisted.

"My only goal over the last two years has been to help him find a way back to his roots and the reason he started off for the glories of city in the first place."

Well, hel—er, dang. The Sister knew what she was about, and it was very clear she had deep affection for Carr. "To prove to his parents that he was worth something," Malina said on a sigh.

"You understand him so well."

"Same goes."

"Frankly, I could use four dozen exactly like him."

"Me, too."

Sister Mary Katherine reached out and grasped Malina's hand in her own. "I've been trying to soothe his soul, but you've healed him."

Malina found the sensation of holding the nun's vein-covered hand disconcerting, but she felt pulling away would insult her. "Oh, ah, well, I don't know about that."

The Sister's face broke in a wide smile. "How lovely."

Malina glanced behind her, and the Sister laughed. "Me? How?"

"That's not what I meant—though you're very attractive and have remarkable eyes. I meant how lovely that you don't yet realize how much you mean to him."

"Who?"

"Carr. He's in love with you."

There was absolutely no answer to that absurd statement.

Sister Mary Katherine tilted her face upward and kissed her cheek, a surprising gesture that brought a glow to Malina's heart. "You'll see. Now, should we go take care of this thieving ring?"

In a fog, Malina led her to the door. Carr loved her?

No. No way. They were having a simple, fun affair, which was bound to end when she was transferred back to FBI headquarters in Quantico, back to the excitement of Washington where she belonged. The good Sister might know her Bible verses and soul-soothing, but she was completely off base about this conclusion.

Wasn't she?

While Malina pondered the implications, she led the nun into Rafton's office. She had no idea if this "secret weapon" plan would work, but she figured they had nothing to lose by trying.

Sister Mary Katherine walked serenely toward their suspect, who immediately stiffened. "Jack, I think we should talk."

As HER COFFEE MUG CLANGED against the others, Malina smiled. "He cracked like the proverbial egg."

Andrea nodded. "The Sister has always had a way about her."

"Her way," Tyler asserted.

Carr sipped from his mug. "Which has worked, by the way."

Sometimes Malina worried that those three were just a bit off center, but since the SAC had complimented her operation and had approved laying a trap for Simon Ellerby, she wasn't about to criticize her investigative team, as unconventional as they might be.

They'd gathered at Andrea and Tyler's house, just down the beach from Carr. Like Carr's place, the back side of the house was mostly windows, but the design and decor were completely different. The modern steel and cool colors were replaced by shades of gold and wood floors, and the curves became more angular and traditional.

The resulting effect was more casual and homey, but Malina greatly preferred Carr's house. Because it was both welcoming and lonely? Or simply because it belonged to him?

She was fighting not to think about Sister Mary Katherine's assertion on Carr's feelings for her. Part of her wanted to panic; part of her wanted to smile.

The rest of her knew she was completely out of her element for the first time in her life.

"So, this ends on Wednesday?" Andrea asked.

Malina nodded. "Based on Jack's information, another shipment of stolen gems—emeralds this time—is coming in early Wednesday morning. After Jack makes his panicked call to his leader, we'll intercept the gems and take them to Simon Ellerby. Ellerby will be forced to deal with us because we have the merchandise."

"Which we'll part with for a small handling fee," Carr added.

"The whole exchange will be recorded by the FBI, who'll be holed up in a van in the marina parking lot." Malina saw twenty different ways the plan could go wrong, but it was still the best opportunity they had. "The merchandise exchange and Jack's testimony will be enough to make an arrest."

"So you'll have Rafton and Ellerby," Andrea said. "But what about the rest of the gang? There are more than two people involved in this operation."

"Oh, we'll get Ellerby to tell us about them. He'll never go down alone. His ego's too lofty."

Andrea looked doubtful that everything would be so simple.

Carr laid his hand over Malina's. "She's pretty fierce in an interview. I don't think getting Ellerby to rat out a few colleagues will be much of a stretch."

Malina shifted toward him and let her gaze linger on his. "We all have our little gifts."

"Great." Tyler stood. "The island will be safe for nuns, children and democracy. Who's up for video games?"

Since Andrea and Carr simply exchanged a silent glance, and Malina had been on this end of one of Tyler's abrupt segues before, she felt it was up to her to ask, "Ah...what?"

Tyler clapped his hands together and headed toward the living room. "Video games. You know, preloaded disks, plastic controllers, simulated action on a TV screen."

"Uh-huh." Sipping coffee, Malina leaned back in her chair. "You guys have fun with that."

"You don't know how to play, do you?" Andrea asked, clearly amused.

"I don't play video games," Malina said, barely resisting a sneer.

Carr cleared his throat.

Knowing he was thinking of the shooting range, Malina glared at him. "I don't play. I train."

"How disappointing," Andrea said as she rose to follow her husband. "Tyler was bragging the other day about this military mission game, and how he could totally kick your butt on it."

Malina flicked a glance at the woman she'd been bordering on considering an actual friend. "Are you trying to distract me from the semidangerous operation that'll take place in less than two days, or are you seriously challenging me?"

Andrea spun, moving her head right, then left. Her blond ponytail swung with each twitch. "Both."

Malina set aside her mug. "I've killed people cuter than you, you know."

"Oh, yeah?" Andrea pulled a plastic pistol—eerily similar to the ones Malina used at the driving range—from a box beside the TV. "Let's see it."

Between her and Tyler's skill and wildly competitive instincts, the game was the most fun Malina had had in a very long time. She didn't relax often. She worked, she thought about work, she slept, ate, then worked again. She couldn't remember the last time she'd done something so normal as play video games. She'd never do this in Washington. She had no friends to play with.

"You're very scary," Carr said as they left via the back door and headed down the beach toward his house.

"The Bureau has an excellent training program."

"And very hot."

"Only for you, Counselor." Grinning, Malina hugged him to her side. "Now let's nail these jerks."

WHEN CARR and Malina stepped aboard Ellerby's boat, the yacht captain was considerably less hospitable than he'd been the first time.

Gone was the mask of the charming party host. In its place was the cold-blooded criminal Carr knew he really was. He'd lost control of his operation, and he wasn't happy about it.

"I thought we agreed you'd come alone," Ellerby said, his annoyed gaze scraping the blonde and disguised Malina.

"Did we?" Making an effort to stay calm and not let

Ellerby's attempt at control rattle him, Carr smiled. "I notice you're not alone either."

Two beefy guys stood a few feet away, looking as if they'd like nothing better than to start the morning with a murder or two.

Carr was counting on both the busy marina and Malina's expert assurance that thieves were generally not killers—except out of panic.

Ellerby wasn't *most* thieves, but if he was panicked, he was hiding the emotion very skillfully.

Their suspect extended his arm to invite them to sit at a small table that was set up on the rear deck of the yacht.

Bold egomaniac.

The FBI's assessment of Ellerby's character was dead-on. Most people conducting an exchange of money and stolen property might do so under the cover of darkness, or at least inside the cabin. Even Jack had made his deals late at night.

Either Ellerby had more ego than sense, or he'd simply been a criminal for so long he'd forgotten his business was completely illegal.

As Ellerby pulled out a chair for Malina, his gaze lingered on her trim, sun-darkened body, encased in a yellow tennis dress. Though Malina smiled brightly at their host, she hadn't been thrilled with Carr's wardrobe choice, but he'd assured her the exposure of her legs was just the sort of distraction they could use.

The dress's short length also meant Carr had to carry her backup pistol strapped to his ankle, which certainly annoyed her more than flashing a lot of skin.

Ellerby sat opposite Carr and next to Malina at the table. "Much as I enjoyed your company at my party, I must admit your call came as a rude shock."

Carr nodded. "I can assure you Jack's blubbering confession about being involved in a major diamond theft provided me the same response."

Ellerby's lip curled in a sneer. "Jack has no appreciation for the subtleties of business."

"You've got a sweet setup here," Carr commented, glancing around.

"Yes, well…" Ellerby's gaze again drifted toward the lovely blonde Malina. "Due to recent events, I'm afraid I'll be moving on soon."

"You're not afraid Jack will go to the cops?" Carr asked.

"And say what?" A hint of a smile appeared on Ellerby's lips. "He has a handful of stones he's trying to liquidate? No, I'm well insulated."

Unfortunately for Ellerby, what he didn't know was that yesterday afternoon, his contact at the diamond mine had been arrested by Australian authorities and was even now spilling all kinds of details about Ellerby's connection.

The FBI was still tracing back the emerald theft that was the source of today's exchange, but when the middle of a structure started to crumble, the rest couldn't be far behind.

"Smart," Carr said.

In response to the compliment, Ellerby merely inclined his head.

Carr had known getting him to talk wouldn't be easy, but he'd anticipated a bit more bragging. Certainly the FBI listening via the recorder Malina was wearing was hoping the same thing. He also noted that the other man kept his hands out of sight, probably folded in his lap. Body language, hands specifically, revealed emotions.

He glanced at Malina to see she was playing her role as vapid girlfriend and simply staring at Ellerby as if he'd recently hung the moon. The devoted look on her face was frankly disturbing.

"As we discussed on the phone," Carr said to Ellerby, "I'm here to merely help out a friend who's gotten into a situation he's unable to handle."

"Yet you expect to be paid for this favor."

Carr nodded. "Naturally. I'm well paid for my expertise in handling troubling situations."

"You have an impressive track record in court."

"Products liability is a lucrative if somewhat mundane field."

"Oddly enough, though, the last few years you've taken on the peculiar challenge of defending churches."

Carr made an effort to look embarrassed. "Yes, well, I got involved in a few projects that weren't altogether legitimate. I thought I ought to lay low for a while. And consulting is both profitable and mostly effortless."

The ease with which Carr slipped into the role of the bored, depraved lawyer made his stomach tighten. After all this time, had he really changed? Was he any different from Simon Ellerby, profiting from the effort and suffering of others?

Malina, as if she guessed his thoughts, distracted him by laying her hand on his thigh. "Baby, are you going to talk boring business all day? You said I could have an emerald."

He let her warmth infuse him. What would he ever do without her? "Of course you can, darling. Let me work out the details, okay?"

As they'd hoped, the idea of selling them one of the gems pleased Simon. The transaction would draw them firmly into the illegality of the operation—they wouldn't tattle to the cops because they were guilty, too.

"Beautiful women are often high maintenance, aren't they?" Ellerby commented.

Malina's fingers dug into Carr's leg, and he picked up her hand, bringing it to his lips. "They're worth it."

Judging by the lightning-quick gleam in Malina's eyes, Carr knew he'd pay for that quip later. Even if it was in character.

With his other hand, Carr reached into his pants pocket and pulled out a small jeweler's pouch, which he dropped in front of Malina. "Pick the one you want." Carr shifted his gaze to Ellerby. "Unless you have a preference, Simon?"

Seemingly indulgent, Ellerby leaned back in his chair. "Be my guest."

With an expression of pure joy, Malina spread the bag's contents on the table. The glittering green stones looked unreal, spread out at random like pieces dumped from a children's board game.

Malina oohed and aahed over several of them, showing each one in turn to Carr. As the indulgent lover, Carr encouraged her to choose the largest, which appeared to be nearly five carats.

Ellerby happily provided a jeweler's loupe for both him and Carr to examine each stone more closely. They haggled back and forth on the price of the stone for "Sandy," then about the transfer fee to give Ellerby the merchandise.

Business complete, Malina leaned toward their suspect, drawing her finger down his forearm. "Did you really steal all these beautiful emeralds?"

Carr's heart slammed against his ribs. That wasn't part of the plan. She was trying to get a confession and cement the case.

Ellerby went statue-still for the space of two of those heartbeats. "Better. I had somebody else do it."

"Wow." Malina's eyes sparked. "That's so cool, isn't it, baby?" she said, rising from her chair, then shifting to Carr's lap. "Thank you for my pretty emerald."

While Carr was fighting the instinctive arousal he always experienced when Malina touched him, she was making a big production out of kissing his cheek and stroking his chest.

With her other hand, however, she was reaching down his leg for the pistol holstered at his ankle.

Almost casual, she rose and turned, pointing the weapon at Ellerby. "FBI. You're under arrest."

In a way, it was all rather anticlimactic.

"Come on, Ellerby," Malina said, her own, commanding voice in full effect instead of the role she'd been playing. "Hands up."

True to the order, Ellerby pulled his hands from under the table and lifted them. In the right one, he held a snub-nosed revolver.

Which he pointed. not at Malina, but Carr.

"You don't want to do that," Malina said calmly, taking a step toward Ellerby before Carr could do anything other than blink.

Ellerby's eyes flashed cold as ice. "Oh, yes, I do. And if you move another step closer, I'm shooting him."

Malina's hot stare seemed to burn right through Ellerby. Then, for a second, she shifted her aim to the guards, who were reaching into their jackets, presumably for weapons. "Don't even think about it."

They ignored her warning, but before they could fully draw their guns, Malina fired off two shots and both men went down.

The whole exchange hadn't taken more than ten seconds.

"You want to try me, Ellerby?" Malina asked, her even-toned voice nevertheless threatening.

True concern crossed the thief's face for the first time. He'd clearly underestimated her.

His hesitation was all Malina needed. She kicked the revolver out of his hand, then jerked him from the chair and forced him to lie facedown on the deck.

Carr rushed over to help her put cuffs on Ellerby, then hauled their prisoner to his feet. Resentfully staring at them, Ellerby groaned in disgust. "A damn blonde bimbo and a puffed-up lawyer."

"Come heavy," Malina said into the watch on her wrist, communicating with the team that had been waiting and listening from a van in the marina parking lot.

"Heavy?" Carr asked.

"You'll see."

Moments later, Carr heard heavy footsteps on the gangway, then a group of agents, dressed in black fatigues and helmets, guns drawn, stormed onto the deck.

Simon Ellerby fainted.

Smiling, Malina jerked off her wig and pushed the thief into the waiting arms of a colleague.

His heart racing both with pride and leftover adrenaline, Carr stared at her. "Thieves aren't violent, huh?"

"He panicked." When Carr continued to gape silently, she added, "He didn't shoot you, did he?"

13

MUCH TO Malina's surprise, less than a week later, the call from D.C. came.

They wanted her back at headquarters in Quantico ASAP, and Carr took her to The Night Heron marina bar to celebrate.

Andrea and Tyler came, as well as Sloan and Aidan Kendrick. Even Sister Mary Katherine stopped by briefly to congratulate her before heading back to the rectory. Carr seemed to be the only one who wasn't in a party mood.

For the past several days they'd lived in an insulated world of accomplishment and blissful satisfaction, and now the bubble had burst.

Malina kept telling herself she was thrilled about the transfer, but part of her was determined to mourn. Carr was a remarkable man, and Palmer's Island felt like a real home for the first time since she'd left Hawaii. She was surrounded by both nature's beauty and people who had carved out their very own slice of heaven.

But her work was her life, and the only way to advance her career was to go back to Washington. She wanted to run the Bureau someday, didn't she?

And yet she only knew two things for certain—she wanted to go, but she didn't want to leave. Since those two states completely contradicted each other, she was pretty well screwed.

Glancing around the table at the people who'd so quickly become trusted friends, dread settled in her stomach. She didn't want to break the bonds she'd made.

But the Bureau would demand a psych evaluation if she turned down this transfer to stay in piddly Palmer's Island.

Plus, in a whole different area of concern, she was desperately trying to convince herself she wasn't turning into her mother.

They were nothing alike. Malina didn't compromise her dreams for men. She wasn't about to settle for ordinary assignments and waste her considerable skills.

She and Carr were only having a fling. The intense feelings would pass—on both sides. Sister Mary Katherine and her vision of love was just that—a hallucination.

But will your skills make you happy?

Carr had spent years using his, and the results made him miserable. Could she really go back to playing the hated game of politics? Had anything really changed except the Bureau's favor?

She glanced at Carr sitting next to her, his thigh pressed against hers as they sat in the booth. He immediately slid his hand over hers, bringing her wrist to his lips, where he pressed a gentle kiss.

But there was no hiding the anxiety in his eyes.

"So, Malina, the bad guys are all safely locked up?"

Sloan Kendrick asked, reaching for another helping of the hot wings in the center of the table.

Focusing on the question instead of Carr's brooding expression, Malina nodded. "The judge even denied Ellerby bail. With his resources and connections, he's considered a major flight risk."

"And the stolen goods?" Andrea asked.

"We found both Jack and Ellerby with paintings, sculptures and gems in their homes, boats and warehouses," Malina said. "We think we've gotten most of the items except the diamonds. There were several that had already been sold to distributors. We're still running them down, but we're not hopeful they'll ever be recovered."

"Are those two goons really threatening to sue the FBI for police brutality?" Tyler asked, looking amused.

Malina snorted a laugh. "I glanced their shoulders. They're lucky to be walking. Drawing down on a federal cop isn't wise."

"I believe you were wearing a skimpy tennis dress at the time, Agent Blair," Aidan pointed out. When Malina's pleased expression turned to a scowl, he added, "But they're obviously sore losers."

Carr squeezed her hand. "She was amazing."

Tyler grinned. "I, for one, admire your accuracy. Sure you don't want to hang around the island and help me scare off the riffraff?"

The casual question evoked an odd response. Every gaze at the table whipped to Carr.

"I belong in Washington," Malina found herself saying after an uncomfortable silence.

Completely contrary to her fearless facade, though, she didn't look at Carr as she said the words.

"COME WITH ME," Malina said to Carr when they were alone in his car—the party pretty much breaking up after her confirmation that she was leaving.

Carr kept a tight hold on her hand, but his gaze was directed at the steering wheel. "I can't."

Her heart lurched. She'd been too impulsive. She'd pushed this too far, too soon. A fling, right? Hadn't she told herself a thousand times that's what this was? Why would he—

"I lost my soul in the city," he said before she could finish her thought. His tortured gaze found hers. "Now that I've found it again, I can't ever go back to that life."

Pulse pounding, she turned toward him, laying her hand alongside his jaw. "Washington isn't Manhattan. It won't be the same. I'll be there for one."

To her heartbreak, he shook his head. "You didn't know me before. You don't understand. I won't be able to resist making connections, working the system."

"It won't be the same," she repeated, though she saw the resignation in his eyes and knew her plea wouldn't help. She even understood why.

He hugged her against his side, as much as the gearbox in the center console would allow. "I was both terrified and hopeful you'd ask this question, but my answer is no. I can't leave this island."

She tucked her head against his shoulder. Their feelings weren't strong enough to make this last. She hadn't done enough to nurture their relationship, and she was choosing advancing her career over his sanity, after all.

But there was one thing she had to know. "Do you love me?"

"Very much," he said without hesitation. "But if I go back, I won't be a man worthy of love."

She wasn't sure a heart could literally break in two, but hers did anyway.

She wanted to tell him she'd stay with him, that she loved him in return, but everything inside her was at war. Her past and present; her career and her life.

"I don't know what I want," she said, knowing she could give him nothing less than her absolute honesty. "I've never loved anybody but my parents. I don't know how it's supposed to feel."

He pressed his mouth against her cheek. "I could give you a demonstration."

SHE LEFT in the early morning, leaving him sleeping in the bed they'd shared the past few weeks.

Leaving the house he'd built, which was so much a part of him, both traditional and modern, warm and cool, past and present, was nearly as hard as slipping from between the sheets and abandoning his body warmth for the unknown future.

She went home.

What choice did she have? Who else could give her answers? Where else could she reflect on her options and choices?

She found her island birthplace the same as always—tourists taking Zodiac raft trips around the cliffs, the annoying buzz of helicopter tours overhead and her parents, welcoming her with open arms, then handing her a surfboard.

Since it was March, the end of winter surf season, the north shore was full of tourists, locals and professionals alike. But, typically, after three days absorbed in the mundane task of renting boards and teaching vacationers to ride the waves, Malina grew restless.

And, though she rarely smiled, her mother telling her she should smile through her sorrow was becoming annoying.

Late in the afternoon of her fourth day home, she walked alone on the beach, watched the deep blue Pacific surf crash against rock and sand, all the while wishing she was at another beach, on another coast and certainly not alone.

Her and Carr's end had been inevitable.

Yet, there were parts of her that were screaming about what a horrible choice she was about to make. Instead of hiding in the bushes, she should be drawing her weapon and firing. Moving forward instead of going back.

"If you wanted to run, you should go over to the track at the high school."

Stopping, Malina turned to see her mother rushing to catch up to her. "I'm not running."

"You're walking too fast to catch all this," her mom said, gesturing at the beauty around them.

"I see it."

Breathing hard, her mom finally reached her. "Do you?"

They were as opposite as night and day—Malina with her dark Thai coloring and her mother's sunny California beauty. Where Malina was edgy, her mother was calm.

Only their eyes were the same. What did her mom see that Malina didn't?

"I met a man in South Carolina," she began abruptly.

"I figured as much."

"You did?"

"Only love can put a look like yours on a woman's face."

Malina cleared her throat. She wasn't sure what to say to that. "Yeah, well, if I accept this transfer, I'll leave him behind. Didn't you say you always regretted giving up Paris and staying with Dad and the surf shop?"

"No, I didn't."

"But—"

Her mom grabbed her hand. "I told you about giving up Paris because I wanted you to think hard about your decision to leave home, to realize that certain life choices can change your path forever, and I didn't want you to feel obligated to stay in a place you obviously longed to escape. I've never regretted my decision. I wanted you to have that same peace."

Peace. Malina was sure she'd never find the same state of mind.

"Besides, my paintings look better on the walls around me than in fancy city galleries. Why do I want to work that hard for someone else's pleasure?"

"A woman shouldn't give up her career for a man," Malina insisted.

Her mom shrugged and hooked her arm around Malina's. "Why not? You break up with a man who makes you unhappy. Why shouldn't you keep one who does?"

"It's not that simple."

"Sure it is. Do you love him?"

"I suppose so."

"Ah, Malina." Her mother shook her head. "You don't suppose anything. You *know*."

Malina stopped and sighed, staring at the retreating waves against the shore. "Yes, I love him." Nothing else could be causing this crazy mixture of pain and pleasure. "But I asked him to come to D.C. with me. He refused."

"Because of you, or because of something within himself?"

How had her mother gotten so wise and perceptive? Artist equaled psychic apparently. "Because of him."

"And Washington is the only place you can serve justice?"

Serve justice. Leave it to her mother to romanticize the FBI, a feat previously thought impossible. "It's the only place I'll move up in the Bureau."

"Do you really want to sit in an office and run the place? No, Malina, you'd be miserable."

"But I want more than…" She trailed off, knowing her thoughts were disrespectful.

"Spending your life managing a beach shop? Oh, honey, there has to be a middle ground between FBI director and surfing instructor."

As she said it, Malina smiled, feeling silly. "Sure there is." And she'd been there for years, but that hadn't made her happy either. Being with Carr, feeling his hand squeezing hers as they walked the beach, as they challenged each other, debated and made love—that had been happiness. "Why can't ambition and love co-incide?" she asked on a sigh.

"They can. The FBI isn't the only place you can right wrongs."

"Leave the Bureau entirely?"

Her mom put her arm around her waist. "You come from a long line of entrepreneurs. Work for yourself. Do what you want, rise as high as you desire instead of going where they send you."

"I could do security consulting," Malina said slowly,

the idea taking on shape and appeal. "That mayor could stand to update his equipment and procedures."

"Sounds like a career to me."

Was her mom right? Was she holding on to false perception? Why was she so determined to look at her mom's decision to give up art school and stay on the island for love as a mistake she'd never make?

Was she really giving up anything? Maybe, instead, she was choosing love over another path.

As for seeing Palmer's Island as mundane, that perception was also off. Her few weeks there had certainly provided plenty of adventure. Working for herself, there was no telling what kind of cases she could get into.

But, more than the excitement, she'd enjoyed getting to know the people affected by her case. She could make a difference to those who mattered to her instead of nameless strangers.

Watching the sun dip closer to the bright blue ocean, she realized something had definitely changed.

She had.

"I'M RESIGNING," Malina said, laying her badge on SAC Samuel Clairmont's desk.

Sam looked up at her, then nodded at the chair in front of his desk. "Have a seat, Agent Blair."

Reluctantly, Malina did as he asked, although even to the end taking orders was difficult for her. Her way was the only way, after all. With a smile, she remembered Carr's accurate assessment of her philosophy.

"Are you looking forward to leaving that much?" Sam asked.

Malina forced a sober expression onto her face. "Sorry, sir. It's been a difficult decision."

"In less than a week, you've gone from the promise

of glory in Quantico to unemployment." Clearly curious, he leaned back in his chair. "Want to catch me up?"

She glanced around his office, the walls full of pictures and commendations. Framed, signed photos of the last three presidents held a place of high honor directly behind his desk.

She didn't envy him anymore. She couldn't care less about glory or running the Bureau.

"I want to open my own security consulting firm." She smiled again. "I'm pretty good at finding lost dogs."

"You're—" Sam shook his head. "You're not serious."

"The dogs would only be an occasional thing, I guess. By staying here, I'll never be anything more than an agent. My career will never advance beyond what it is now."

"It's still a pretty damn good job, and you're one of the best. And stop smiling like that. You're scaring me."

"I'll try." And she did. Mostly, though, she wanted to get this meeting over with and go see Carr. She needed this part of her life finished, so she could start down her new path. "I appreciate your confidence in me, sir, but I don't have the patience for politics anymore."

"And this has nothing to do with Carr Hamilton?"

"Oh, it has everything to do with him."

"If you're staying here for him, you can still work for me. I'll talk to the director about canceling the transfer."

She let her gaze rove the wall of honors. "The Bureau doesn't hold the appeal it once did."

Sam turned briefly to see what held her fascination. "I

know you don't need us, our commendations or probably our paycheck—you'll have a wealthy husband."

Malina's heart jumped at the idea of marrying Carr. She hadn't gotten *that* far planning her new path.

Still, the idea didn't seem as crazy as she might have considered a few weeks ago. She pressed her lips together to keep from grinning.

"I'm asking you to stay because *we* need *you*," Sam said forcefully.

"You didn't like my plan for catching Simon Ellerby," she pointed out.

"I reluctantly approved the operation, but since it worked, you seem to have been right. I'm not going to say we'll always agree, but give me a chance to make it work. And here in Charleston we're not as backwater as you might think. We have the harbor assignments and a SWAT team, you know."

Either of those assignments would certainly feed her desire for adventure. But she wasn't sure Carr would love the idea. She'd have to consult with him before she could agree to join the team.

Wow, they really were a couple.

"You're doing it again."

She bit her lower lip. "Sorry."

"At least give it a few months."

Maybe she was being rash in leaving the Bureau. She did respect and admire Sam. And since closing the Ellerby case, her coworkers had abruptly cut off the ragging about dog-napping.

As if sensing she was wavering, Sam leaned back in his chair. "I notice you didn't turn in your gun."

Malina laid her hand protectively over her Glock. The sidearm was as much a part of her as her hand. She could buy her own, but how many opportunities other than the firing range would she have to actually use it in the private sector?

As she started to slide the weapon from its holster, Sam held up his hand. "Keep it for now. I want you to talk to some people before you decide." He picked up the phone and said, "Send them in."

Malina glanced out the office windows to see the mayor and his twins walking through the bullpen.

What the— She whipped her head back toward Sam.

"The mayor asked me to contact him the minute I heard from you," he said. "I called him and told him about our appointment today."

Malina rose as Mayor Parnell walked into the office. "Good afternoon, sir, I—"

Madison and Edward threw themselves against her sides. "Don't go!" they cried in unison.

"Well, I don't—" Malina began.

"What'll we do if somebody runs off with Pooky again?" Madison asked, blinking tears from her bright blue eyes.

Malina thought it would be churlish to point out she and her brother had been the last ones to roll out that dastardly plan.

"There's this big kid at school that threatens to punch me if I look at him," Edward said, his voice desperate. "Who's going to help me with that?"

Ah, your dad's big, bad bodyguards?

Malina looked desperately at the mayor for help.

"Sorry, Agent Blair. I told them about your transfer to Quantico." He sighed. "I had a moving speech all planned to convince you to stay. It appears that won't be necessary."

Sam rose, and now he was smiling. "I'm sure it was

an excellent speech, Don. Maybe you can use it at Agent Blair's commendation ceremony."

Good grief. Malina finally understood how Simon Ellerby had felt being taken down by a bimbo and a lawyer.

"Look, kids," she said, kneeling between them. "I'm not going anywhere. I'm still deciding my career plans," she added, her gaze flicking to Sam. "But I promise I'll be around to protect you guys and Pooky."

Then, contradicting her uncertainty, and in between patting the twins on their backs, she caught the badge Sam tossed her.

"CARR, YOUR BOAT'S BEEN broken into."

Prior to picking up the phone, Carr had been seated at his desk, staring out his office window. At this news from the sheriff, however, he jerked to his feet. "When? How?"

"I have no idea," Tyler said. "Al Duffy just called me. I'm headed over to the marina now. Why don't you meet me?"

"I'm coming."

He hung up the phone and strode from the office, telling his secretary that he had to go out for a while.

Since waking up last week to find Malina gone, he'd been going through the motions of waking, working, sleeping. He'd struggled over the promises he'd made to himself—and Sister Mary Katherine—and the irresistible lure of being with the woman he loved.

Could he really live in a city like Washington, full of high-profile clients and power brokers, and not indulge in old habits? Was there any lure left in trying to prove his parents had been short-sighted in leaving him behind?

Yes. And no.

Besides, Malina was assigned to Bureau headquarters in Quantico, Virginia. He could buy a house with a farm, grow peaches or cotton and retreat to the beach on weekends.

Peaches or cotton? he asked himself as he pulled into the marina's parking lot.

Okay, maybe not.

But there were certainly plenty of charities and foundations in the Washington area that could use his expertise.

Bypassing The Heron, he jogged down to the pier. At four-thirty it was a bit early for after-work cruisers to be about, but he did expect Tyler and Al. He saw neither of them. He could see the tip of *The Litigator* bobbing in the water some distance away.

What in the world was going on?

Could the would-be thief have actually overpowered both men? And why? Still, the whole incident had Carr's nerves clanging with alarm. Was there another member of Simon Ellerby's thieving ring that they'd been unaware of?

His body braced for anything, he moved closer. He wished like crazy for a weapon and paused as he realized he'd left his phone in the car. But then, Tyler had undoubtedly been wearing both his police radio and his pistol, and he didn't appear to have fared so well.

Two slips from his own, he saw the smoke.

A stream was billowing out an open window, so, thief or no thief, he broke into a run. He leaped onto the deck, flung open the door and nearly plowed into Malina, who was frantically waving a towel over a pot on the stove.

His heart literally stopped. *"You* broke into my boat?"

he asked, his gaze frozen to her trim figure, encased in jeans and a cherry-red shirt.

She scowled. "I was trying to make you a romantic dinner."

She was? He could hardly believe she was real.

"Al Duffy is an ass." She stalked across the cabin to open another window. "He claims he saw me sneaking around. He knows I know you. But does he walk up and ask me what I'm doing? *Nooo*. He calls the sheriff. Then Tyler shows up, gun drawn I might add. We nearly shot each other!" She pointed at him, as if the whole mess was his fault. "I spent fifty bucks on seafood at your buddy's shack in the marina's parking lot. He's wrong, by the way. You don't just throw everything in the pot and let it boil."

Carr had barely heard her rant and continued to stare at her as if she were a mirage. "You were making me a romantic dinner?"

She flopped on the sofa. "As you can imagine, Tyler laughed like a loon about that before he left. He offered to send Andrea over to help. I probably should have taken his advice."

Now that Carr was convinced he wasn't hallucinating—'cause, hey, in his fantasies he always pictured Malina in a bikini and her deep blue eyes full of lust, not frustrated and upset—he caught the implications of her appearance.

She was back.

But for how long? Was she making him a goodbye dinner? If so, she was going to find losing him much more challenging than she'd expected.

Carr leaned over the pot. He saw crabs, shrimp, sausage, corn, potatoes and onions, but no liquid. "Did you add water?"

She looked puzzled, then rueful. "I was so distracted by nearly murdering the sheriff, it's entirely possible I screwed up the instructions."

"We can probably salvage it." He dumped the food into another pot, tossed out the burned bits, which turned out to be mostly potatoes, then reached into the fridge for a beer. He poured the contents of the can into the fresh pot, along with several cups of water.

Turning to face her, he leaned against the counter. "When did you get back?" he managed to say.

"Late last night. I slept all day, then came here."

A bout of nerves he hadn't experienced since his first middle school dance washed over him. "Oh, yeah?"

Her eyes cleared, the anger gone. She blinked as if just realizing he was there. Standing, she moved toward him.

He noticed she wore not only her pistol and holster, but her badge, which was tucked, shield out, in the front pocket of her jeans. "Is this an official visit?"

"Sort of."

He frowned. Something about her was different, not the least of which were her vague answers. "When do you go to D.C.?"

She stopped inches away from him, and his heartbeat picked up speed. "I'm thinking of doing an HRT refresher course next month."

"I see." But of course he really didn't. "I wasn't sure you were coming back here."

"You're here," she said simply.

He finally realized what was different. The change was subtle, but up close he could see the distance in her eyes was gone. The vague suspicion and doubt she'd used as a barrier between them had disappeared. Hope sparked deep inside him.

"I learned something important at home." She curled her arms around his neck.

"The weather's too perfect in Hawaii?"

"No, but it is."

"The surfing is lousy."

"No, it definitely isn't." She laid her finger over his lips before he could ask any more inane questions. "I learned this is how love feels. At least for me."

He crushed her against him so hard that tears exploded behind his eyes. "You're not going."

"I resigned."

"But you're wearing your badge."

"The SAC talked me into staying, at least for now. We'll see how things go, then decide together what to do."

"My money's on Sam."

She leaned back. "Not we—Sam and me. We, as in you and me."

Carr planted a hard, relieved, hopeful kiss on her lips. "I love you."

"And I love you. Nothing in my life is as important as you."

Carr searched her gaze, seeing the truth of her conviction. He knew the happiness flooding him was only beginning, and the future would be faced, not alone, but with her. "I thought your job was your life."

"Not anymore."

"Does my house have anything to do with your decision to stay?" he teased.

"I *do* love your house," she hedged.

Laughing, Carr hugged her. "We'll move you in tomorrow. And remind me to call Charlie McGary and have him call off the Virginia search."

"The Virginia search?" Malina asked.

He moved to the couch, where he sat and tugged her into his lap. "Charlie's my real estate agent."

Her eyes widened. "Wow. You weren't afraid of the temptation to go back to the Dark Side?"

"I figured I'd have a high-ranking federal law enforcement officer to keep me on the right path."

"Yes, you would."

He cupped her cheek in his hand. "You're my life. I couldn't let you go without me."

"Carr?" she asked as he brushed her cheek with his lips.

"Yeah?"

"You still talk too much."

"I bet I can fix that." As he kissed her, he poured all the love and promise he'd been holding quietly inside for so long. Neglected as it had been, his heart overflowed with gratitude.

Unfortunately, the next thing he heard wasn't a chorus of angelic approval, but Al Duffy's scratchy voice.

"No more mopin' around. You hear, boy? Ain't dignified for a man to be so depressed about a woman who can't even cook."

LATER, LONG AFTER DINNER and sunset, Malina lay in the master cabin's bed, her head pillowed on Carr's bare chest just as she had the first time they'd been together.

That night the sea had undulated beneath them, rocking them in a steady cradle of contentment, even as she'd convinced herself she was simply releasing stress from her demanding job. Tonight, the waves continued their relentless motion, and she was completely different.

She could finally appreciate fulfillment with the love of her life. She didn't have the constant drive to wonder what professional challenge might be over the next horizon. She didn't worry about what compromise might cost her.

At last she understood her mother's internal peace.

Still, she wasn't her mother in many ways.

She turned on her side and propped her head in her hand. "I still think Al Duffy was being difficult, not—as you so innocently believe—trying to get us together."

He mirrored her pose. "It seems imminently obvious that he saw you, worried you wouldn't stay long enough for me to see you, knew how much I needed to see you, so he took matters into his own hands. Drastic matters maybe, but still pure of heart."

She snorted in derision. "Oh, please."

"You two are going to have to find a peaceful middle ground eventually. Al's a good guy down deep."

"Way down."

"Maybe so, but he does know everything about this area. He can navigate through these waters, under any weather conditions, with his eyes closed."

"I can shoot accurately with my eyes closed. Who'd you rather have in a fight?"

He paused. "I think you've won your argument, Agent."

"Of course, I have. But do you know what became of Simone Anderson?"

"The abrupt segue of the day award goes to…"

She slapped his chest lightly. "Come on, Simone Anderson."

His eyes darkened with regret. "She was my client for the case against Nelson Chemicals. Most of her family was poisoned by the runoff water from their plant."

"You remember her?"

"I've had a lot of free time on my hands the last week. You might say I took a walk down memory lane."

"And did your stroll reveal where she is today?"

"No." He slid his hand across her hip, drawing her closer and confirming what she'd thought—he was afraid to know too much. Another case like Bailey Industries was too painful to face.

"Simone works for an international peace organization that strives to eliminate river and stream chemical poisoning produced by industrial plants in third-world countries."

Carr went still, then shook his head as if trying to clear his thoughts. "She what?"

"You heard me. She credits you with opening her eyes to the neglectful policies that run rampant in countries without a legitimate legal system. How about Bruce Carmandy?"

"Who? I—" He stopped, and Malina could clearly see his brain straining to switch gears. "He was paralyzed by a bus hitting him on Seventh Avenue in New York City."

"By a bus driver who had a serious history of drug abuse. With his settlement money from the city, Carmandy got a great apartment overlooking the East River and paid for the driver to go through rehab yet again. Apparently the treatment stuck this time. The two men started a company that builds motorized wheelchairs."

His eyes full of wonder, Carr stared at her. "How did you find out all this?"

"I investigated. I'm highly trained, you know."

"I know. But why?"

"To show you that your debt is paid. You don't have to redeem yourself anymore. You've made mistakes, but the good completely outweighs the bad." She slid her fingers through his silky hair, letting her gaze rove his beloved features. Beaches, oceans and sunsets included, she'd never tire of that view. "You're a great man. Not just in my eyes, but many others."

"Thank you." As she felt a deep breath of relief escape his chest, he kissed her lips, then trailed his mouth along her jaw.

Carnal sensations that had shifted briefly into dormancy reasserted themselves. She inhaled his sandalwood-scented cologne and knew this was the place she belonged for the rest of her life.

"Is this 'you're redeemed' thing just a ploy to keep me from butting into your cases?" he whispered between kisses.

"I refuse to answer that question on the grounds it might incriminate me."

He held her tightly against him. "I love you."

"Same goes, Counselor. Same goes."

* * * * *

COMING NEXT MONTH

Available September 28, 2010

REQUEST YOUR FREE BOOKS!

2 FREE NOVELS PLUS 2 FREE GIFTS!

HARLEQUIN®

Blaze

Red-hot reads!

YES! Please send me 2 FREE Harlequin® Blaze™ novels and my 2 FREE gifts (gifts are worth about $10). After receiving them, if I don't wish to receive any more books, I can return the shipping statement marked "cancel." If I don't cancel, I will receive 6 brand-new novels every month and be billed just $4.24 per book in the U.S. or $4.71 per book in Canada. That's a saving of at least 15% off the cover price. It's quite a bargain. Shipping and handling is just 50¢ per book.* I understand that accepting the 2 free books and gifts places me under no obligation to buy anything. I can always return a shipment and cancel at any time. Even if I never buy another book, the two free books and gifts are mine to keep forever.

151/351 HDN E5LS

Name	(PLEASE PRINT)	

Address		Apt. #

City	State/Prov.	Zip/Postal Code

Signature (if under 18, a parent or guardian must sign)

Mail to the **Harlequin Reader Service:**
IN U.S.A.: P.O. Box 1867, Buffalo, NY 14240-1867
IN CANADA: P.O. Box 609, Fort Erie, Ontario L2A 5X3

Not valid for current subscribers to Harlequin Blaze books.

Want to try two free books from another line?
Call 1-800-873-8635 or visit www.morefreebooks.com.

* Terms and prices subject to change without notice. Prices do not include applicable taxes. N.Y. residents add applicable sales tax. Canadian residents will be charged applicable provincial taxes and GST. Offer not valid in Quebec. This offer is limited to one order per household. All orders subject to approval. Credit or debit balances in a customer's account(s) may be offset by any other outstanding balance owed by or to the customer. Please allow 4 to 6 weeks for delivery. Offer available while quantities last.

Your Privacy: Harlequin Books is committed to protecting your privacy. Our Privacy Policy is available online at www.eHarlequin.com or upon request from the Reader Service. From time to time we make our lists of customers available to reputable third parties who may have a product or service of interest to you. If you would prefer we not share your name and address, please check here. ☐

Help us get it right—We strive for accurate, respectful and relevant communications. To clarify or modify your communication preferences, visit us at www.ReaderService.com/consumerschoice.

HB10R

HARLEQUIN®

A *Romance*

FOR EVERY MOOD™

Spotlight on

Inspirational

Wholesome romances
that touch the heart and soul.

See the next page
to enjoy a sneak peek from
the Love Inspired® inspirational series.

*See below for a sneak peek at
our inspirational line, Love Inspired®.
Introducing HIS HOLIDAY BRIDE
by bestselling author Jillian Hart*

Autumn Granger gave her horse rein to slide toward the town's new sheriff.

"Hey, there." The man in a brand-new Stetson, black T-shirt, jeans and riding boots held up a hand in greeting. He stepped away from his four-wheel drive with "Sheriff" in black on the doors and waded through the grasses. "I'm new around here."

"I'm Autumn Granger."

"Nice to meet you, Miss Granger. I'm Ford Sherman, from Chicago." He knuckled back his hat, revealing the most handsome face she'd ever seen. Big blue eyes contrasted with his sun-tanned complexion.

"I'm guessing you haven't seen much open land. Out here, you've got to keep an eye on cows or they're going to tear your vehicle apart."

"What?" He whipped around. Sure enough, mammoth black-and-white creatures had started to gnaw on his four-wheel drive. They clustered like a mob, mouths and tongues and teeth bent on destruction. One cow tried to pry the wiper off the windshield, another chewed on the side mirror. Several leaned through the open window, licking the seats.

"Move along, little dogie." He didn't know the first thing about cattle.

The entire herd swiveled their heads to study him curiously. Not a single hoof shifted. The animals soon returned to chewing, licking, digging through his possessions.

Autumn laughed, a warm and wonderful sound. "Thanks,

I needed that." She then pulled a bag from behind her saddle and waved it at the cows. "Look what I have, guys. Cookies."

Cows swung in her direction, and dozens of liquid brown eyes brightened with cookie hopes. As she circled the car, the cattle bounded after her. The earth shook with the force of their powerful hooves.

"Next time, you're on your own, city boy." She tipped her hat. The cowgirl stayed on his mind, the sweetest thing he had ever seen.

*Will Ford be able to stick it out in the country
to find out more about Autumn?
Find out in HIS HOLIDAY BRIDE
by bestselling author Jillian Hart,
available in October 2010
only from Love Inspired®.*

"I've thought of nothing but you since yesterday," Carr rasped in her ear

Different didn't even begin to describe the hunger pulsing through her. She'd anticipated a spark with their kiss and gotten an inferno.

Malina pressed her lips to his throat and buried her hand in the inky locks of his hair that indeed felt like silk. "You're part of my case. I shouldn't—"

He silenced her with another kiss. Her protests died in the wake of the raw emotions consuming her. She craved his touch, knowing instinctively he could drive away the loneliness and satisfy both her body and her mind.

She wanted his skin pressed against hers. She wanted to let loose the fire behind his dark eyes.

His hand slid up her stomach, and her breasts tingled in anticipation. But before he could reach his goal, his thumb brushed her shoulder holster....

Blaze

Dear Reader,

My hero in this story, Carr Hamilton, was inspired by, well, a car. The Triumph Spitfire was a British two-seater sports car manufactured from the late sixties to late seventies, and I drove one—painted British Racing Green—as a teenager. (If I can find a picture, I'll be sure to share it on my Web site.) It was the coolest thing on four wheels, and I just couldn't resist giving it to Carr to tool around Palmer's Island.

I also had to give my charming hero a heroine to challenge and confound him. Malina Blair is the extreme of me—tough, fearless and always ready with a comeback. (In real life, I admit avoiding confrontation whenever possible, have a ridiculous, irrational, frustrating fear of heights, and the only kind of gun I can fire with any skill uses water instead of bullets.)

Come to think of it, I'm probably not like Malina at all. But then this is the world of romance, and we can all escape for a while and be anybody we want to be.

Hope you enjoy!

Wendy Etherington

P.S. Additional apologies to the hardworking folks at the FBI Field Office in Columbia, SC. I moved their office to Charleston for the purposes of my story.